MORE DEATHS
THAN ONE

MORE DEATHS THAN ONE

Marjorie Eccles

A CRIME CLUB BOOK
DOUBLEDAY
New York London Toronto Sydney Auckland

A CRIME CLUB BOOK
PUBLISHED BY DOUBLEDAY
a division of Bantam Doubleday Dell Publishing Group, Inc.
666 Fifth Avenue, New York, New York 10103

DOUBLEDAY and the portrayal of a man
with a gun are trademarks of Doubleday,
a division of Bantam Doubleday Dell
Publishing Group, Inc.

Library of Congress Cataloging-in-Publication Data

Eccles, Marjorie.
More deaths than one/Marjorie Eccles.—1st ed.
in the United States of America.
p.   cm.
"A Crime Club book."
I. Title.
PR6055.C33M67   1990
823'.914—dc20   90-22795
CIP

ISBN 0-385-41918-X
Copyright © 1990 by Marjorie Eccles
All Rights Reserved
Printed in the United States of America
July 1991
First Edition in the United States of America

1   3   5   7   9   10   8   6   4   2

B54 1747

The quotations at the head of each chapter are taken from *The Changeling,* the play by Thomas Middleton and William Rowley.

MORE DEATHS
THAN ONE

ONE

"Vengeance begins;
Murder, I see, is followed by more sins."

THE DAY WAS DYING as the hare ran home through the stiff, frosty fields. He came to the forest and though timid of men he raced along their tracks, his powerful haunches propelling him with primordial instinct towards his form and his mate. Then he felt, rather than heard, the thrum of hoofbeats behind him. Ahead he smelt blood and corruption and laid his ears back. His exophthalmic eyes swivelled, but fear pushed him forward towards the man in the parked car.

It used to be considered unlucky, and still is by some, to have your path crossed by a hare. Old Wat had run this way once before, but the man was past caring about that. He was indifferent now to luck, either good or ill.

The day was also John Culver's seventieth birthday. A day for celebration, no doubt, had there been anyone to celebrate with.

A little thing like that was unlikely to bother him, though. He wouldn't have remembered it was his birthday at all if he hadn't received that single card, he told himself, almost believing his own lie.

Happy Birthday to a Dear Father it said in gold letters on the front, the words she couldn't bring herself to write. Inside, the single name, Georgina, quickly scrawled as if she might soon regret the impulse that had caused her to acknowledge him for the first time in seven years. Just Georgina. Not Georgina and Rupert, she'd had enough sense for that. His face darkened as he stood by the edge of what Evelyn had always insisted on referring to as the lake—though it wasn't in all conscience much more than a large pond with a rocky outcrop in the middle that she'd called the island—his shoulders hunched like some old brooding cormorant as he stared out across the water and nourished thoughts of the man he had spent several years of his life hating.

But despite this there was a warmth stirring inside him again, which took no account of the harsh bitter wind that slapped the water at the margin of the lake against the little skiff he used for fishing, and whistled round the grey stone house on the mound behind him. John Culver, for the first time since Georgina had gone off with that bastard, felt he had reason for hope. He pushed aside the thought that in some odd sort of way the card, breaking the silence, had shamed him. Beneath the triumph that after all *she'd* been the one to give in was a feeling he was doing his best to ignore, that in some inexplicable way he'd been diminished.

The sun was going down in a cold flare of red against a pale green sky. There'd be a frost again tonight. He was a strong old man, fit for anything, nothing wrong with him except for a bit of creakiness in his knees, but there was no sense in staying out here too long in the cold. It slowed up his reactions and his movements. He'd missed the hare because of that, and missing his quarry was something he rarely did. He whistled to Minty who was running round the edges of the lake, her belly low to the ground in true collie fashion, tail between her legs. Shouldering his shotgun, he walked stiffly back towards the house, shivering despite himself. The cold spears of the daffodils that spread every year beneath the birches here by the lake had taken one look at this spring and decided to go no further for the moment. Most of the huge old Atlantic cedar with its dark sheltering branches which had stood firm for years on the windward side of the house had gone down in one of the wild storms of the winter, making the house look lopsided, giving it a naked, unprotected appearance that he couldn't get used to. The rooks were nesting again in the old walls of the ruined tower they'd colonised, and cawed bad-temperedly as the wind hindered their work.

He took a diagonal route across the grass, feeling it already crisp under his feet, and Minty, sheep-dog trained, brown and white with light untrustworthy amber eyes, kept at his heels until suddenly she stiffened and let out a sharp bark. Culver turned and saw a car coming up the long drive, an unusual enough occurrence to make him pause and watch. His heart began to knock at his ribs. Georgina?

TWO

"A master sin, imperious murder."

IN DEATH, the man in the Porsche was seen to be tall and slimly built, with dark brown, longish hair, dark hairs sprinkling his forearms, nicotine stains on his fingers. There was nothing much else left to tell what he'd looked like in life. The shot had been fired at close range and his face was missing.

He was wearing a heavy dark blue woollen sweater and jeans, and a Rolex Oyster on his wrist. His fashionable grey suede jacket had been thrown onto the seat beside him and was now spattered with the rusty stains of dark, dried blood. He had fallen half across the steering wheel. The shotgun lay on the floor of the car which had been parked in a small clearing under the beeches in the forest, away from the road which wound through it but just off the chief ride where horses were regularly galloped. It had been a late afternoon rider going home who'd found him: a woman, who'd dismounted to point out the notices forbidding parking and got more than she bargained for.

There'd been no real attempt to hide the car, other than the fact of it having been driven away from the road. The immense old trunks of the beeches grew tall and close but afforded little actual cover, even in summer when thick with foliage, since their branches grew high. Now, on this bitter March evening the forest known as Scotley Beeches was bare and even in the dusk the scarlet car stood out like a beacon. Powerful lights had been strung up around it, making a stage-set in the surrounding darkness and from a distance the policemen moving between the trees had an unreal air, like figures at the beginning of a pantomime scene: another part of the forest.

One more car joined those already assembled round the edges of the clearing, their blue lights slowly revolving. A young plain-clothes sergeant unfolded his skinny length from it and walked quickly over to the centre of the scene, where Dexter and the Scenes of Crime team, closely watched by the Detective Chief Inspector, Gil Mayo, were doing their best within the constraints imposed by the close confines of the car and the necessity not to touch the body. Every now and then, brighter lights flashed as Napier took his camera shots from every conceivable angle.

"I came as soon as they rang," Kite told his chief, stamping his feet and waiting for his briefing, reckoning on Mayo already having the situation weighed up. Never a man for snap judgements, unlike Kite, the D.C.I. should all the same have made his own observations by now and decided what needed to be done. He was leaning against the trunk of one of the beeches, arms folded, frowning at nothing in particular. A big, dark, sparely-spoken Yorkshireman, quiet and determined, with a strong, uncommunicative face, he had a vitality and energy about him, not at first apparent but making itself felt when it came to making decisions.

"Thanks for coming in, Martin," he said, looking up and giving Kite the benefit of his smile, rare enough for the sergeant to guess Mayo was aware of the size of the favour he'd been asking. Not liking having to ask, either. Nevertheless it *was* a smile, lighting grey eyes that could otherwise be disconcertingly cold in their regard, especially to those at the sticky end of the law. "Spoilt your leave, I'm afraid, but it would've meant calling somebody in from outside —or throwing Farrar in at the deep end. Hope you weren't doing anything special."

Kite shrugged in a so-so manner. If Mayo wanted him it wasn't his to question why, though Farrar wasn't likely to be feeling over the moon about it. Sweating on the promotion which was in his own opinion long overdue, a chance to prove himself, and the gaffer calling in Kite off leave! Kite sympathized, but not a lot; he'd been in the same position himself and it hadn't done him any harm in the long run.

"You weren't, were you?" Mayo quizzed. "Doing anything special? Hadn't planned to take Sheila out or anything?"

"Nothing that mattered. Only being self-indulgent."

Some slight economy with the truth here, but never mind. The

reality was too boring to interest anyone else. Seizing on the chance
of a comparatively slack period at the station, Kite had decided to
make headway into at least some of the time off due to him, promis-
ing Sheila he'd make a start on the long-awaited do-it-yourself extension to the back of the house and give some time to the kids. And
instead he'd been forced to spend his entire leave crouched in front
of the fire nursing a streaming cold and aching limbs, bored out of
his mind, his eyeballs burning with reading too much and his ears
ringing with too many aspirin. Now, his cold almost over, he felt
slightly guilty at the alacrity with which he'd jumped at the chance
to come back. No point anyway in beginning on the extension work
with only two days of his leave to go, he'd told Sheila, avoiding her
eyes.

"Bit of a cold as a matter of fact," he admitted, feeling some
explanation was needed but not elaborating. Not much point really.
Mayo, who'd nobody to please but himself, since his own wife was
dead and his daughter had flown the nest to make a career for herself, might understand about the domestic stress but would certainly
feel it was up to Kite to cope with it. Which he would, of course.
Two hours ago he wouldn't have given much for his chances of
being able to knock the skin off a rice pudding, but the call out had
pumped the necessary adrenaline into him. Surprising where it came
from when you needed it. "I'm okay now," he said, bracing his
shoulders to show himself capable of anything.

Mayo gave him a sharp look. "Let's hope you are. Don't want you
passing out on us."

"No fear of that." Kite jerked his head towards the car. "They told
me there's some bloke shot himself, that right?"

Without comment, Mayo waved Kite towards the Porsche, which
had been carefully hauled backwards for several feet clear of the area
in which it had rested. That place was now taped off and would be
thoroughly and minutely gone over in the morning when it was
light. There was little point, he'd decided, in wasting time and re-
sources until his searching men could see what they were doing
properly.

Approaching the car, Kite had a word with Dexter, who stood
back to let him view the interior. Hands in his pockets so that he

wouldn't accidentally touch anything, he thrust his head in, smelt first the stench, then saw the shotgun and the bloodied, clotted mess that had been the head. "Christ!"

Thick frost was already riming the tree trunks and in the clearing the stiff dead bracken sparkled as though sprayed with Christmas glitter. Beech mast and leaf mould made a thick, springy mat underfoot. The air felt as though you were breathing razor blades. Kite took in several lungfuls and wondered briefly if he hadn't seriously overestimated his recovery rate.

Regarding his sergeant quizzically, Mayo restrained himself from making any remark. He had a lot of time for Kite who was able, shrewd and cheerful—and not ambitious enough to be about to kick his chair leg from under him. Besides, his own initial reaction had been precisely similar to Kite's, only no one had been there to observe it. However experienced you were, however many mangled corpses you'd viewed before, the first glimpse of the next one was always a nasty experience. And Kite, resilient as he was, was obviously not up to the mark tonight. Despite his assurances he was looking decidedly peaky. Though give him his due, he was almost visibly getting a grip on himself.

"Any idea who he is?" the sergeant asked.

"Not yet. But we've already been on to Swansea. They ran the registration number through the computer and came up with a Rupert Fleming. Presumably that's him. It's a local registration and Spalding seems to think he's seen it around."

Kite nodded. There weren't all that many Porsches in Lavenstock. "No note?"

"Stuck on the dash. Take a look."

Mayo handed Kite a small plastic envelope through which could be seen a leaf torn from a yellow self-stick memo pad. The handwriting, though far from illiterate, was disjointed and difficult to decipher. Resembling a kind of shorthand, it looked like the hand of one whose thoughts ran faster than his pen, possibly made even more illegible in the present case by haste or despair. The message was brief: *I've had enough. I'm packing it in. Sorry it didn't work out.* It was signed, *R.*

Poor devil, had been Mayo's first thought on seeing the note.

What hopelessness and anguish brought anyone to this mess? But that had been before he'd really looked, before Ison had spoken.

Kite seemed to pick up his thoughts. "Doc Ison been yet?"

Mayo informed him, his breath coming cloudy on the freezing air, that the doctor had been and gone. "He left an emergency at the Cottage Hospital when he got the call to come here and he's slipped back to see how things are while we're waiting for Timpson-Ludgate." Not that he needed to come back. He'd certified death and that was all that was strictly necessary, and some would have been content to leave it at that, packed their bags and been off, sure of their fee. But Ison was cut from a different cloth.

Timpson-Ludgate was the pathologist and the significance of his being sent for wasn't lost on Kite. "Not suicide, then?"

"Somebody wants us to think so."

"What about the note? Not easy to fake a fist like that . . . hello, here is the doc. And talk of the devil, His Nibs an' all." Kite had spotted another, very recognisable car arriving close behind the police doctor's sedate blue Vauxhall, the elderly gleaming Rover belonging to the pathologist.

"About time. We've hung about long enough." The doctor climbed stiffly out of his car and approached the Porsche. "Everything all right at the hospital, Doc?"

"Nothing to worry about now. Mother and baby both doing well."

Funny job, his. Violent death one moment, birth the next, in its way just as violent but concerned with all that mattered, really, the essentials of life, its beginning and its end.

"Evening, Mayo, evening young Martin!"

This was the pathologist, following close on Ison's heels, scattering greetings around like largesse, eminent enough to be affable with everyone, especially those not in a position to contradict his pronouncements. "Bit nippy for this sort of thing, but at least it'll keep the flies away, eh? Hm, more than an hour or two since *he* shuffled off this mortal coil!"

The last part of this was muffled, issuing from inside the Porsche, into which he had already plunged his head, clearly not expecting a reply, which was perhaps just as well in view of Mayo's expression.

They didn't come better than Timpson-Ludgate when it was a question of his job. Moreover, anyone prepared to tackle one like his could be forgiven a lot in Mayo's opinion . . . but he found this morbid humour, peculiar to doctors, pathologists and policemen, hard to take at times. All right, it was one way of coping with the vile and sordid muck they all had to deal with, but God, there were limits!

He suspected Ison was another who didn't care much for it either. A sensitive and humane man underneath the reticent medical exterior, he lifted a shoulder before turning away to begin a token grumbling to Kite about the inadequacy of the lighting. "Can't expect us to examine him very thoroughly in these conditions, Sergeant. A few more lights wouldn't come amiss."

"I'll see the D.I. about it." Kite went off to find George Atkins.

"Cheer up, we'll do our best, Henry, as always," Timpson-Ludgate answered the doctor breezily, withdrawing his head to address Napier. "Finished with your photographs, sonny? Okay, but don't go away, I shall need you." Turning to Mayo, he said, "If you've anything else to be doing meanwhile, I should get on with it. We shan't be finished here in five minutes."

"I know, I know, but I need a statement from the woman who found him and I'd like to have a look at that jacket before I go, as soon as you've finished with the body. I want to confirm who he is."

"No problem, you can have it once your man's got some photos of it for me and I've had a dekko. Not going to be easy, the state he's in, you know." The pathologist nodded to Napier, who adjusted his lens and began flashing the video camera again. Atkins, walking with his elephantine tread, came across with a couple of technicians and started superintending the erection of more lights. Mayo thrust his hands into his pockets and counselled patience to the inner self clamouring to get on with the job.

"Thanks. If you want me, I'll be over by the S.O.C. van but I'm going to take a look round the back first. Martin?"

The sergeant accompanied Mayo as he walked round to the back of the Porsche, following the delineated access path, keeping clear of the taped-off area. There had been heavy rain the previous week, which had left soft mud under the frost of the last two nights, but the springy layer of beech mast covering it had precluded the possibility of finding any footprints. The weight of the car, however, had sunk clearly visible tracks.

"Driven in from the Lavenstock end by the look of it," Kite remarked.

"And only one set of tyre marks—so either somebody had a long walk back or there was another car. Nothing immediately apparent in the vicinity."

"We'll spread the search out in the morning," Kite promised. "Who was it found him?"

"A Mrs. Salisbury. Lives at Fiveoaks Farm over yonder." Mayo gestured in the direction of the entrance to the woods. "She'd been riding when she found him—so she carried on home and telephoned us from there. They've told her to stay where she is until we've seen her, which'll be midnight at this rate. He stamped his feet again and looked impatiently across the clearing. "Trouble with these bloody medics, they think we've got nowt else to do but wait till they've done their stuff," he said unreasonably. "Let's give 'em a poke."

But it was some time before the pathologist was ready to talk to them. At last he beckoned them over, still kneeling by the body, which had now been lifted out of the car. He heaved himself to his feet as the three policemen approached, all taller men than he— Mayo big and formidable, Kite with his long whipcord thinness and Atkins, bigger than either, large, solid and dependable. "Doubtless you had a good look before I arrived so you'll not be surprised when I tell you it wasn't suicide."

Mayo looked at Ison, who nodded at this confirmation of what they'd thought. Timpson-Ludgate went on, "Couldn't have done it . . . not unless he had arms four feet long. To make *that* sort of mess of his face, the shot would have had to be fired from two, two and a half feet away. At a rough estimate. If it was self-inflicted, I'm a Chinaman. No contact wound. Very little spread of pellets."

"Can you hazard an opinion about the direction of the shot? The angle?"

"From the right, getting him full in the face. The exit's on the back of the skull and most of the loose matter and damage to the car's on the far side, not towards the back. Angle of entry . . . from slightly above."

"So he must've been looking towards his killer, then, through the window?"

"I'll say nothing so definite as 'must' at this stage. I'd prefer to reserve certainties until I've had him on the slab. And until ballistics have had their say." He relented. "All right, work on the assumption that he's been murdered. For the rest—probably somewhere in his thirties, apparently in good condition, though what his lungs are like is another matter," he said, indicating the stained fingers, "and you'll have to wait for the post mortem to find that out. Not that it'll make any difference to him now, poor bugger," he finished cheerfully. "I'll fit him in tomorrow, get the full report to you as soon as possible."

"When did it happen?"

"I'm not prepared to be too specific about that either at the moment, with the weather as it is. Say, eighteen to twenty hours."

Mayo did a quick calculation. "Some time late last night then, or early this morning? Hm. And what's the *other* thing anyone might be doing out in this God-forsaken spot at that time on a cold and frosty night like last night? Can't see this as a crime of passion."

"Me neither," observed Kite, shivering.

"Well, that's your problem, you're the investigating officer. Myself, I've nearly done, here at any rate. We'll have him away in two ticks, but as far as I'm concerned you can get at the car now."

As they waited for the jacket to be lifted from the passenger seat, Mayo warned the other two, "We'll keep what T.-L. says under wraps for the present. If someone's been at pains to fake this as a suicide, we'll go along with that until it's confirmed otherwise. Say nowt, both of you, but keep your ears and eyes open. All right, Martin, let's see what we've got."

The jacket handed over, Kite began on the pockets. "Looks as though we're in business." A brown leather wallet, with the initials R.G.F. stamped in gold across the corner. In the wallet a driving licence, issued to Rupert G. Fleming of 22, Baxendine House, Lavenstock.

"So it *was* his own car," Mayo said. "Baxendine House next port of call then, after we've seen Mrs. Salisbury at the farm. It's one of those new blocks of flats by the river."

The wallet was also found to contain a chequebook, one five-pound note, the usual selection of credit cards, a ticket stub from the local theatre for a performance a few weeks earlier and a snapshot tucked into one of the compartments. From the trouser pockets had come a handful of small change.

"Where's his keys, Nick?" Mayo asked Spalding.

"Here. They were in the ignition, sir."

"I don't mean the car keys, he must have had house keys and so on."

But no others had been found.

Mayo held the snapshot by the corner under the lights and saw a young couple with two children, probably under school age. Before tucking it into a plastic envelope and then into his own wallet, he studied the photo, particularly the face of the man he took to be Fleming. An unusual, arresting face, high-cheekboned and with a full, sensual mouth that had something of arrogance about it, a touch of the Florentine princeling, the sort of face that looked out haughtily from the chiaroscuro background of a Renaissance portrait. The young woman was plump and dreamily smiling, with a mass of dark hair falling to her shoulders. The picture had been taken in spring—there were daffodils in the background—and she was wearing flat, open sandals, a long flowered skirt and a grey shawl. One of the children was hugging a stuffed toy kangaroo. A moment of family happiness. A man, you'd have said, with everything to live for.

A pattern of stars and a new moon showed through the black lattice of the bare branches, cold and remote, investing the bizarre scene with even more unreality. Mayo swore softly to himself. At this point in an investigation he was always painfully aware of his need to come to terms with his own feelings of inadequacy. How to explain the eruption of violence into ordinary family life . . . how to justify the trust put in him to bring the perpetrator to justice? No answer to that but to pitch in, muck or nettles.

The murder weapon was being lifted carefully into the S.O.C. van. A twelve-bore, double-barrelled shotgun, both barrels of which had been fired, it had now been photographed from every possible angle in relation to the body and its position on the floor of the car, measurements had been taken, sight lines established and the weapon carefully lifted, labelled and wrapped.

"What else have we got, Dave?" Mayo asked the fingerprint man.

"Definite set of dabs on the steering wheel and the gear lever, sir, and on the gun, but nowhere else at all, not even on the door handle."

Which seemed to indicate the murderer had been too anxious to get rid of his own prints and had neglected to impose the victim's on the door handle as well as the other places Dexter had mentioned.

"I'd be a lot happier," Dexter said, "if it didn't appear to have been gone over with a nit comb, wiped over inside and out—and been through a car wash as well, I shouldn't be surprised. Not much else we can do until we've got the body bagged up and moved, sir. The forensic lads might get more after they've been over it at the garage. Looks as though they're taking him away now."

The man's hands had already been encased in polythene and the head treated with similar care in case there should be lost any more of what remained of the victim's shattered flesh and bone and brains, what the pathologist had so delicately termed "loose matter." Now, what remained of Rupert Fleming was zipped up and carried into the waiting mortuary van.

As the van was driven off, Mayo handed the dead man's jacket over to Dexter. Curiously, it hadn't absorbed that taint of corruption which had been so overwhelming in the car. It smelled rather pleasant in fact, of soft supple suede and a masculine whiff of expensive aftershave. Something was puzzling Mayo about the smell of that jacket, but for the moment, since he couldn't think what it could be, he was obliged to be content with making a mental note of it, pigeon-holing it for further reference in a mind that rarely forgot anything completely.

THREE

*"How lovely now dost thou appear to me!
Never was man dearlier rewarded."*

UNDER THE MOON, snowdrops glimmered palely in great drifts beside the path to the front door of Fiveoaks Farm and a breath of their cold honey scent wafted towards the house as Mayo and Kite waited for an answer to their ring.

The door opened, revealing an entrance hall that was large and low-ceilinged, with an agreeable air of having been furnished and cherished and comfortably lived in ever since the house was built, three or four hundred years ago. The unsmiling young man with the ruddy, outdoor complexion, conservatively dressed in a soft blue woollen sweater and cords and who said he was Tim Salisbury, had been expecting them but didn't appear to be overjoyed about it. A vague mutual antipathy passed between him and Mayo as Mayo's own brand of instant shorthand summed him up: Thirtyish. Archetypal prosperous young farmer. Young Tory. Features reminiscent of the young Duke of Kent. Maybe not a lot in the upper storey, but sharp and wary.

"I suppose you'd better come through," he said, "Susan's in the other room," adding, in what Mayo thought a decidedly patronising manner, "I hope you realize what a terrible shock this has been to her . . ."

"We'll do our best not to upset her, Mr. Salisbury."

Prominent blue eyes stared back with patent hostility. "Let's hope you won't."

He led them across the stone flags, past a Jacobean open carved staircase, and turned the door-knob of a warm, lamplit room, where a big log fire burned on the hearth. A Christmas card sort of room, old oak furniture gleaming with a patina of age and polish, brass and copper shining, apple logs and beeswax scenting the air. It was big and low-ceilinged, running almost the full width of the house, and though it was not noticeably tidy, with books and magazines scattered around, and children's toys forming an obstacle course to the chairs they were offered, it spoke of the care lavished upon it, and nothing was lacking in the way of modern comfort and amenities.

The young woman who sat up with a start as they entered and swung her legs to the ground from the broad, chintz-covered sofa seemed unlikely on the face of it to be the one directly responsible for the upkeep of the room. She looked like no farmer's wife Mayo had ever seen. Not by any stretch of the imagination could you see her getting down to it with polish and Brasso, not even in rubber gloves. Those white hands with their pearly-pink nails looked as though they'd never lifted a duster in her life. He was well aware that he might be doing her an injustice and stereotyping her in a way that would have infuriated his daughter Julie—but the conclusion was inescapable, looking at her.

She was a beauty—and there weren't many you could honestly say that about, the human race being on the whole a pretty undistinguished lot in Mayo's opinion. Mrs. Salisbury was the exception that proved the rule. Not simply good-looking, but beautiful in a delicate, ethereal way that owed much to her colouring. She had that dazzling fairness of complexion which, though the English are supposed to be a fair-skinned race, is rarely seen on these shores. A yellow sweater that might have made many women look sallow gave a radiance to her skin like a light shining through alabaster. Her hair was a pale silver-gold and fell in loose shining waves to her shoulders. He thought of Curly Locks in the nursery rhyme, who was invited to sit on a cushion and sew a fine seam, and feed upon strawberries, sugar and cream. Then he met a disconcertingly appraising gleam in the luminous blue eyes trained on his face and admitted wryly that Julie would have been right to criticise him for jumping to conclusions. There was intelligence there, astute enough to preclude any suggestion of vacuousness.

"This is Detective Chief Inspector Mayo, darling, and Sergeant Kite." Tim Salisbury was looking at her as though he couldn't believe his luck in having married her. "If you think you can manage it . . ."

"Oh. Oh yes, they said someone would be along. Sorry, I must have dropped off. That brandy you gave me, Tim . . ."

She excused herself for not having changed from her riding clothes. She'd been too shattered. The boots had been removed but she still wore her jodhpurs and the high-necked yellow sweater. Lifting her hair with the back of her hand, a gesture that revealed the contours of her breasts under it and only just escaped being theatrical, she exclaimed, "Goodness, is that the time? The children . . ."

"It's okay, they're in bed and asleep. Katie saw to them before she went."

Susan Salisbury smiled wanly at her husband, subsided back onto the sofa and stared at Mayo. The huge eyes suddenly brimmed with tears that didn't, however, spill. The small straight nose quivered slightly but didn't even turn pink. Her husband sat beside her and put his arm protectively round her slim shoulders.

"This hasn't been a very pleasant experience for you, Mrs. Salisbury, but I'm afraid there are some necessary questions I must ask," Mayo began.

She clasped her hands together with slightly conscious courageousness. "I shall have to face them sooner or later, I suppose. Is there, do you think, Tim lovey, a smidgin more brandy?"

Salisbury leaped to refill the glass she extended, which she accepted back as homage due to her. Kite shifted on his chair. He wouldn't have said no to a heartening smidgin himself, but none was on offer, either because Salisbury had heard and believed that police officers weren't supposed to drink on duty, or because he wasn't drinking himself and didn't see why they should. Kite consoled himself with the scarcely less-satisfying spectacle of Mrs. Salisbury disposed on the sofa instead.

"Would you like to tell me in your own words what happened?" Mayo was asking.

"Well, I was on my way home—"

"At what time?"

"The time when—when I saw the car, you mean? It was half past four, within a few minutes either way. Katie, the girl who looks after the children for me, usually leaves at ten to five to get the bus home, so I was keeping an eye on the time. As I passed the clearing,

Magister dug his heels in, in fact he nearly threw me . . . he was trembling and refused to go any further. So I turned him round to take the other way home and then I noticed the car was still there."

"Still? So you'd seen it before?"

"I thought it had to be the same one I'd seen from the top of Merrett's Hill. There's strictly no driving through the forest but people do, you know, on the bridle-paths . . . Well, anyway, I was curious to know why it was there and I was prepared to tell them off . . ."

He could believe it. The attractive, husky voice was quick and educated, she had an imperious manner not all that far underneath her present distress. "Then"—she took a gulp of brandy—"well, that was when I realized whose car it was."

"You recognised it?"

"Oh yes, didn't I say? Yes, I knew it was Rupert Fleming's Porsche as soon as I reached the clearing. And when I looked in, I—oh God, it was only a second, but I recognised him straightaway."

Mayo said sharply, "How did you know it was Rupert Fleming?"

She stared at him and then as she slowly comprehended the meaning of his question she became ashy pale, whiter even than the natural pallor with which Nature had endowed her. She began to tremble. Mayo knew this was how it took witnesses sometimes, when they actually began to realize the import of what they'd seen. Delayed shock, but genuine, he could have sworn. There was no play-acting this time. And he had just been thinking—God forgive him—that she had almost begun to enjoy the drama of her part in the tragedy.

Tim Salisbury threw an angry glance at the two policemen. "Sue darling, you don't have to go on with this."

"Better get it over with, Tim." She swallowed, blinking back tears, determined to be brave and show herself as cooperative. She *was* being a much better witness than Mayo had at first feared. Pretty sharp, really. "Well, look," she said now, "you don't recognise people simply from their faces only, do you?"

Mayo conceded the point to a certain degree. But how well had she known Rupert Fleming—if she'd been able to know instantly who he was from such a quick appraisal of general build, hair colour, even from that fairly distinctive suede jacket of his? On the other hand, she'd known the car. She would have expected, if anyone had been inside it, for it to have been him.

He said, the blunt Yorkshire copper he chose to be on certain occasions, "I'm a bit behind you, ma'am. Who is—was—Rupert Fleming, apart from being a friend of yours?"

"Oh, I wouldn't say a friend." A little colour had come back into her cheeks. "It's his wife Georgina that we know, isn't it, my love? And she's not exactly a *friend* either, just someone my sister went to school with. Someone I've known for ages. She was Georgina Culver."

She spoke as if the name was too familiar, or well-known, to need explanation and Mayo searched his mind, wondering where he'd come across it before. Kite helped him out, speaking for the first time from the unobtrusive position he'd assumed to take his notes, and with the advantage of his local upbringing. "Culver's Haulage, ma'am?"

It was Salisbury who answered. "That's right, only John Culver's sold out now. Pity, it wasn't a bad sort of business, I suppose," he added, looking down his high-bridged nose, "but I heard Culver did well enough on the deal and, after all, there are no sons to carry it on, only Georgina . . ."

Husband and wife didn't look at one another, or speak, but something was being said between them. Salisbury finished, rather quickly, "I don't think he stirs much out of that old barn of a place where he lives now that he's retired."

"And where's that?"

"Next door to us." Mayo wryly acknowledged this was not meant in the suburban sense, since there was not, to his knowledge, any other dwelling within half a mile either side of Fiveoaks Farm. "His property marches with ours. He used to let out a few acres to my father but then he suddenly decided he was going to start farming himself when he retired. As far as I know he's never even begun."

Salisbury's tone had become more truculent as he spoke, his already ruddy outdoor complexion intensified, his collar appearing suddenly tight. He had the short, thick neck and the high colour that indicated he'd have to watch his weight and his blood pressure as he got older, a stiff, guarded young man with that sort of bluster and uptightness that often conceals a basic uncertainty. "I've offered to buy the land," he went on, "but he's absolutely not interested, not at any price, stubborn old fool."

"I guess he wouldn't have kept up that feud with Georgina so long if he hadn't been . . . stubborn, I mean," his wife said.

"Susan, what's that got to do with it?" The question was flat and uninflected, but something in it—a warning, perhaps?—alerted Mayo.

"Why nothing, I suppose, darling," she admitted with a smile, "but they're going to hear sooner or later, I imagine."

"What feud is this?" Mayo knew he was expected to ask and he did because the answer interested him very much.

"Oh, it was all too Gothic for words," she explained lightly. " 'You marry my daughter and neither of you will set foot over my ancestral threshold again!' Or words to that effect."

"Some ancestral home!" Salisbury put in. He became all at once informative, seeming just a little over-anxious to keep the conversation going his way. "Bought it lock, stock and barrel from the Paulings, who'd lived there since the year dot, when the old girl died. Culver's a self-made man—made his pile buying up army surplus and scrap metal after the war and went on from there." He didn't bother to hide his fourth-generation contempt for someone so ungentlemanly as to have actually made his own way up in the world, rather than have had a privileged lifestyle handed out on a plate, plus the wherewithal to continue it.

"What did he have against Fleming?"

After the slightest suggestion of a pause, Salisbury's wife shrugged and said obliquely, "We hardly knew Rupert, as I said, and Georgina's not one to exchange confidences."

"Especially since you're not exactly friends," Mayo reminded her.

"No," she agreed, eyeing him rather sharply. "Not since she married."

"What did Rupert Fleming do for a living?"

"He was some sort of journalist, I think."

"Local paper?"

"No, I believe he was a freelance."

"Not very well known," Salisbury commented, then, showing a rather belated sympathy, he asked, "When was he murdered, poor devil?"

"Murdered? Who said anything about murder, Mr. Salisbury?"

An unreadable expression crossed his face. "Well, wasn't he? God, you mean it was suicide?" he asked Mayo, who thought it better to leave the question unanswered.

Mrs. Salisbury had given a soft cry of distress. "Oh Tim, what did you think? He *must* have shot himself . . . if you'd seen . . . but *why?* You'd have thought he'd everything to live for. He was young and good-looking and—oh, it's too horrible to think of!"

So she'd noticed. However horrified she'd been by her discovery, she'd looked long enough to see the gun on the floor, the suicide note stuck on the dash, to draw the inferences.

At that moment a little mewling cry started up from somewhere near the fireplace, like a kitten or the bleat of a lamb, making Mayo realize that he'd been aware for some time of strange little snuffling noises coming from the same corner. He saw now that a baby alarm was installed there, and the noise issuing from it was the relentless demand of a small baby.

Susan Salisbury had jumped up, not, Mayo thought, without relief. "You must forgive me, that'll be Clarissa. I'll see you when I come down."

"Just one question before you go, Mrs. Salisbury. What were you doing last night?"

"Me? I was in bed. I had a very bad headache, and I went to bed about nine o'clock."

"And you, Mr. Salisbury?"

"I had an N.F.U. meeting."

"What time did it finish?"

"I don't really remember, it was very late, I suppose it was after midnight when I got home, but what the hell's that got to do with anything? What does it matter what *we* were doing? We've got nothing to do with all this."

"Just checking, sir," Mayo said blandly, "just checking." The baby's cry was working up to panic proportions and Susan Salisbury was growing fidgety, as any mother would. "I don't think we need any more from you at the moment, Mrs. Salisbury. We'll have your statement typed out and perhaps you can come in and sign it sometime tomorrow. Good night to you, ma'am."

Before she went out she paused, framed becomingly in the doorway. "If there's any way we can be of further help . . ."

"Thank you, Mrs. Salisbury, I appreciate that offer."

She acknowledged this gracefully and went out.

There had been undercurrents stirring in that room which he hadn't understood, Mayo thought as the husband escorted them to the door and closed it firmly behind them. Susan Salisbury, like her furniture and her house, was cherished and perhaps more than a little spoilt. Evidently her husband adored her and she adored being adored. Nothing wrong in that, if that was how their relationship worked, but he wondered if it wasn't a little too obvious, and momentarily why a woman as intelligent as he felt she was should ally herself with someone as irredeemably stupid as Tim Salisbury appeared to be.

And he also wondered about her and Rupert Fleming, an entirely intuitive supposition, neither evidential as yet, nor even perhaps justifiable, but one which he didn't intend to ignore.

"It wouldn't do any harm to have a poke around and see if there's ever been anything between Mrs. Salisbury and Fleming," he told Kite when they'd left. "I should think that's a very long shot, and it may have nothing to do with this if there was, but I think it's worth following up. Salisbury was a bit cagey. I should think that's a natural condition with him, but he strikes me as the sort who could be jealous as hell."

"With a wife like that, who can blame him?" Kite said.

FOUR

"Pray resolve me one question, lady."
"If I can."
"None can so sure. Are you honest?"

LONG BEFORE that first death occurred Alex Jones had been aware of something seriously amiss in her sister's life, though the cause of it had to be largely speculation, since Lois was naturally secretive, never speaking much about her private life with anyone. Latterly, not even with Alex. That's what being a police sergeant did for you, it lost you the trust of your friends and sometimes family, even of the naturally confiding ones. And Lois had never been that.

"She's quite capable of sorting herself out, so relax," Mayo said. But he knew that this worrying was just Alex being Alex, something she couldn't help. She couldn't bear situations she couldn't do anything about; she had an inborn compulsion to sort them out. It sometimes got her into trouble, occasionally upset people, and created a variety of conflicting emotions in Mayo, ranging from exasperation to an amused tolerance, because he knew he'd never change her. "Can't see what you're bothering about," he told her, "she'll work things out her own way."

"Nor can I, really," answered Alex, frowning. "Just that things don't seem right, somehow. Nothing you can put your finger on . . . little things. You know, suddenly buying all those new clothes she doesn't need. And she bit my head off when I said that new haircut didn't suit her."

"Well, it doesn't. Same cut as yours, but it makes her look scraggy." He grinned, not really joking. The short, sleek haircut suited Alex's clear profile, gave her that clean-cut, cameo look that went so well with her creamy skin, showed off the good shape of her head and the irresistible curve at the back of her neck—but not Lois.

"Scraggy! For goodness sake don't let her hear you say that! No, she's upset about something and it's making her quite waspish."

"What's new?"

"Come on, that's not fair, Gil."

And it wasn't, really. Piquant rather than waspish, you'd have said if you were being truthful. Amusing with it, but not lately.

"It has to be a man, of course."

"Surprise, surprise," rejoined Mayo, who was prejudiced. For some time he'd been convinced that Lois was behind Alex's determination not to marry him, knowing as he did of Lois's aversion to marriage on principle. She egged Alex on in her fight to keep what she saw as her independence, he was sure . . . but that was only one of her attitudes that irritated him. He was irked by what he thought was her pretentiousness, was wary of her sharp wit.

And she was the only woman, apart from his mother, who insisted on calling him Giles.

Lois, who ran an interior decorating business with great success and élan, was not so lucky in her relationships with men—and there had been quite a few, apart from her divorced husband. Unlucky, or wanting something most of them couldn't live up to. Alex wasn't in any position, however, to criticise on that score. The sisters didn't always pick their men well, either of them, though for different reasons.

There wasn't much to go on at all, really. But it bothered Alex.

And then the body of Rupert Fleming turned up and the whole of the Lavenstock police force, including the uniformed branch, were so busy that worries about Lois were forced to the back of her mind.

It was the finding of Fleming's body, and the need to inform his next of kin, which was now propelling Mayo towards the town. It was part of his job and he'd lost count of the times he'd had to perform this particular task, but he still detested it, especially where children were likely to be involved. He hated the thought of the trouble and anguish in store and the thought of being the instrument of it didn't do much for his self-esteem. The ancient Greeks, when they had killed the bearer of bad tidings, might have had a point, he reflected sardonically.

In an effort to avoid thinking deeply about what would never cease to be an ordeal for him, he sat back in the car as he was driven towards Baxendine House and let his thoughts drift. But rather than concentrating themselves on the case, as they should have done, he found them floating towards Alex. He blamed the scent W.P.C. Jenny Platt was wearing, delicate but disturbing in the close confines of the car, reminiscent of one Alex sometimes used. They'd stopped to pick her up at the station in case she should be needed and she sat in the back seat, pretty, curly-haired, young and smelling delicious. Tough as they come, in spite of that, a capable young woman who expected no favours because of her sex.

Alex had the same sort of attitudes—and yet he at least knew how vulnerable she really was. Especially in that one area that was closed to him, the subject Alex was disinclined to discuss, knowing how he felt about it. It never ceased to amaze him that she could sort everyone else out but couldn't, or wouldn't, do the same for herself. Especially when it concerned that Irishman, that Liam, he thought bitterly, the ex-lover in her life, who wouldn't remain ex. A man who wouldn't let an old love die a decent death and yet wouldn't do anything to resolve the situation hadn't got much going for him in Mayo's book. Lately, however, he'd had a feeling, quite unsupported by any evidence, that Liam might finally have quitted the scene. Why, Mayo didn't know, because Alex certainly wasn't saying. Nor where to, either. He could have jumped in a lake, flown to Australia or gone to the devil. All three for all Mayo knew, or cared.

"Yes?"

The woman who answered the bell regarded the three of them unsmilingly, suspiciously eyeing W.P.C. Platt's uniform.

"We'd like to speak to Mrs. Fleming, please," Kite said.

"I'm Georgina Fleming."

She wasn't the woman in the photograph.

She was taller for one thing, and where the other woman had been dark and full-figured, with her hair in a curling mass on her shoulders, this one was slender to the point of thinness, a narrow, taut figure, her light brown hair fashionably bobbed and crimped and frizzed like a rag doll's. She was wearing a belted cream silk tunic with a high neck over a short, straight black skirt that revealed long slim legs in sheer black tights. Also, an impatient expression.

"What is it you want?"

Mayo explained who they were and that he wanted to speak to her about her husband, and at last she seemed to understand that she would have to let them in. Abruptly, she told them to follow her.

She lived in one of the smart new warehouse conversion flats that had been built overlooking the river, on land that had once been heavily industrialised but was now cleared and landscaped with groups of young trees and flowering shrubs and flowerbeds at present filled with crocus. Winding through it was a man-made stream fed by the Stockwell itself, that you crossed by means of little bridges and which gave to the complex a feeling of being built on an island, and perhaps to the residents a superior feeling of insulation from the busy everyday life of the town which went on behind them. The flats were regarded as upmarket housing in Lavenstock, with prices to match. Mayo had once thought he would have liked to have owned one of them and been disappointed to find them beyond his means —or at any rate beyond what he was prepared to pay.

Now, in the long living room of this one, he turned away from the big blank expanse of the uncurtained window—the second-floor flat was on the side of the river and wasn't overlooked—realizing with a feeling of having escaped that this sort of place would never have suited him, much less Alex. It was too impersonal, it had no sense of ever having seen years of life lived in it, despite what the architects called "retention of distinguishing features." Translated, this meant, he supposed, an excuse for keeping the intrinsic parts of the old warehouse it had once been, interesting when it came to the pointed arch shape of the window, but not necessarily in the exposed central heating pipes and the two enormous metal structural supports which ran floor to ceiling through the middle of the room.

Perhaps it was also the way in which it was furnished, no expense spared but in total contrast to the warm, comfortable, lamplit room they had just left. Severe modern lighting, a polished parquet floor with one or two Persian-type rugs, and the rest of it all chrome and glass, in monochrome black and white except for the leather seating, which was a bright shocking pink. A tall square glass vase containing three silk lilies stood on the black glass coffee table and there was a collection of white Lalique on a bookcase. Blown-up surrealist black and white Man Ray photographs decorated the walls, the one called "Glass Tears" over a fireplace into which was set an unlit modern functional electric fire—no flickering flames, real or imitation, here.

All very tasteful, no doubt, but equally uncompromising. The central heating was switched on and the room was warm, but there was a chill pervading it that had nothing to do with the temperature, that surely emanated from the cool, brisk Mrs. Fleming herself.

"You'd better sit down."

Her tone was pretty chilly too. She made no indication where they might sit and Kite chose an upright C. R. Mackintosh-type ladder-back chair with an exaggerated length of back which looked, and was, extremely uncomfortable. Mayo sank inescapably into the sighing embrace of pink leather, opposite Mrs. Fleming. Curly-haired Jenny Platt, wiser than her superiors, chose a camel-saddle stool at the end of the room to perch on.

The fact that Kite had warned Georgina Fleming there was serious news about her husband didn't seem to have shaken her unduly. In fact it was a long time since Mayo had seen anyone so self-possessed in any circumstances. Perhaps the meaning hadn't penetrated, or he hadn't been specific enough. Or perhaps she didn't care.

Maybe she knew already.

Mayo kept a close, careful watch on her as he spoke. She was a good-looking young woman, around thirty, palely made up, her mouth painted poppy-red, not beautiful in the way Susan Salisbury had been, but her looks were the sort which would serve her well into old age. There was no softness about her to crumple or blur the fine edges. In profile her face was sharp, her eyebrows were shapely and well defined above curiously clear eyes, tawny-coloured, with a dark rim around the iris and thick, dark lashes.

Not wanting there to be any mistake this time, Mayo told her in plain words that her husband had been found shot dead in his car, where he had apparently been since the previous evening. There followed a long silence. She still showed no visible emotion. If she hadn't indeed been prepared, Mayo reflected, she was the coldest fish this side of the Antarctic.

"Where?" she asked finally. "Where did you find him?"

Where? The question was unexpected. Most people reacted with disbelief, or horror, or shock. They burst into tears. They wanted to know how. And why. He reminded himself that at a time like this anyone's actions were likely to be unpredictable—thought was rarely rational—and told her he'd been found at Scotley Beeches.

"Scotley Beeches?"

"That's going towards—"

"Oh, I know where it is," she interrupted. "It just seems a peculiar sort of place for him to choose."

She'd immediately assumed, either innocently or otherwise, that Mayo had meant suicide, though he'd never mentioned the word. He didn't correct her.

"This might not be easy for you to answer—but can you think of any reason *why* he might have wished to take his own life, Mrs. Fleming? Did he have any problems?"

She shook her head vehemently, the Raggedy Ann haircut swinging round her face, but she seemed less certain. "Why does anyone?"

"Had he any worries?" Mayo pressed.

"Not really."

"Nothing at all?"

"Well, he wasn't too happy about his work."

"What was his job?"

"He was a freelance journalist." With seeming reluctance, after a few more prods, she informed them that he'd been doing it for about a year. It had been difficult, what with unions, and most papers having staff writers, and God knows what else. He'd done several features for the county magazines and some reviewing, he'd reported on local theatre productions, but it hadn't amounted to much and he'd been talking of giving it up. "It must have been worrying him more than I thought."

"Perhaps."

By the time this case was over, the dead man would have become a person to him, Mayo thought. He would have talked to those who had known him in real life, made his assessment of his character and, if he were lucky, found out why he'd been murdered. But now at the beginning, he was just a name, a body which had been horribly done to death, and he was casting around for a peg to hang the enquiry on. Which in the nature of things was most likely to be his relationship with his wife, and maybe the rest of his family. "Tell me a little bit more about your husband, Mrs. Fleming. What was his background? Was he local?"

No, she said, he'd actually been born in India. Patiently, little by little, like drawing teeth, he extracted from her the information he wanted. Rupert Fleming's father, it appeared, had worked for an oil company in various parts of the Far East and Rupert and his brother had been sent home to boarding schools for the children of parents living abroad. His parents, now retired, lived in Derbyshire. Rupert had been destined as an accountant but had failed the exams. He'd tried his hand at a career in photography, then in insurance, one or two more things, but nothing had worked. That's why he'd decided to try journalism. After that, she lapsed into silence.

"Did he own a shotgun?"

Her eyes flickered at the abrupt change of subject. "No. I doubt if he'd know how to use one . . ."

"Mrs. Fleming, is this your husband's handwriting?" Mayo held out the torn-off memo page so that she could see what was written on it.

After a moment she said tonelessly, "Yes, that's Rupert's writing," and stood up.

Thinking she imagined the interview was at an end, he said quickly, "There are still a few more questions about your husband that I'd like you to answer."

"Is that necessary?" She took a cigarette from a new unused pack on the mantelpiece and sat down again, but without lighting it.

"It's routine, in any case of violent death, to enquire into the deceased's affairs and his last movements and, with your permission, look through his effects."

"Surely not when it's—suicide?"

"We have to be satisfied."

"In that case, I suppose I must." She looked at him with unconcealed dislike.

Mayo thought, you've no option, lady, and let the look slide off him. It was his job to be suspicious, to probe, to stick his nose in

where relatives—and he—would rather not, to ask awkward and im-
pertinent questions, never mind what anybody thought.

The first question he had to ask was when had she last seen Fleming.

It had been on Sunday evening, and no, she couldn't say where he
had been during the time since.

"Was that usual? I mean, for him to be away from home and for
you not to know where he was?"

"He often had to be away when he was working on a story."

"Suppose you had to contact him in an emergency?"

"What emergency? Look, we're both busy people. I run my own
business management consultancy, which means I'm often away too,
and his movements were never very certain. Trying to give precise
details in those circumstances could lead to confusion."

He was beginning to get a picture of their marriage. Two people,
pursuing separate careers, hers the more successful of the two. In all
probability with separate lifestyles, too. He hadn't asked about children, he didn't think he needed to. With the sort of life they led,
children were unlikely to be on the agenda. He took out the photograph that had been in Rupert Fleming's wallet and handed it, still
in its protective polythene, to his wife. "Was this your husband?"

She looked at it for several moments before passing it back. "Yes."

"Do you recognise the other woman?"

Though he could hardly have phrased that less tactfully, he was
sure by now that was just what the girl in the snapshot was: the
other woman. For a moment he hoped for Mrs. Fleming's sake that
she might be able to say it was some mutual friend or relative, his
sister perhaps, but she replied unemotionally, "I've never seen that
person in my life."

"Have you any idea who it might be?"

"No."

She was lying, but any woman in similar circumstances might have
done the same, and he didn't feel he need press her at this juncture.
He went back to Sunday evening. Fleming had been away during the
previous week but had then appeared unexpectedly, it seemed, read
the Sunday papers and then cooked a meal while she was still busy
with some weekend work she'd brought home. Cooking was one of

the things he'd liked to do, while she hated it, and he'd made one of his special vegetarian dishes and opened a bottle of wine to go with it.

She hesitated as she came to the point where they'd finished the meal, colouring very slightly, and for a split second her whole taut body seemed more pliable, the poppy-red mouth soft and full. They'd made love, Mayo thought. She'd known about the woman in the photograph, even if she'd been keeping to the strict truth in saying she'd never *seen* her, even if she suspected that Fleming was going to her later that evening, but it hadn't made any difference. Was this what they called an open marriage, each taking lovers as and when they fancied? It never seemed a particularly sensible way to carry on to him, seeming to deny the honesty it was meant to proclaim. Why make the commitment to marriage at all if this was how you felt? Why play with fire?

Later, about nine o'clock she thought, he'd left. He'd told her when he arrived that he had a meeting arranged with someone unspecified.

"And he didn't come home afterwards?"

"No." The curious amber eyes were wide and unblinking. She looked him straight in the eye. Nor had he said when he'd next be back. She hadn't seen him since.

He felt dissatisfied with the interview, but it was probably as far as he could profitably go at this point and, after extracting himself with some difficulty from the clutches of the leather chair, he stood up.

He thought, from his assessment of her, that Georgina Fleming wouldn't shrink from identifying the body, but with the scene of carnage in the car still fresh in his memory, he decided he wouldn't inflict that on her unless he had to. Was there anyone else, any other close relative, who could undertake this and spare her the ordeal? he asked. She told him there was no one except Fleming's elderly parents. She would identify him herself, she said coolly, as soon as he wished.

"That's up to you, Mrs. Fleming. I do realize it's very late, and we can leave it until tomorrow—"

"I have a very heavy day tomorrow," she interrupted crisply. "I'd prefer to get it all over with tonight."

Did she, too, he wondered, weep glass tears?

But when she looked down at the body of her husband stretched on the mortuary slab, she reacted after all very much as anyone else might. Since there was nothing left of Rupert Fleming's features to identify, she couldn't look at his face and say this was him, this was my husband, but as Susan Salisbury had said, you don't know a person by his face only. Especially a husband.

As she looked down at the body, her face took on a greenish pallor, beads of sweat broke out on her forehead. He thought she might be going to faint and took her elbow. She tried to speak and found herself momentarily incapable of doing so, a classic symptom of profound shock.

"Mrs. Fleming, is that your husband, Rupert Fleming?"

Her nod and the barely uttered yes which she managed sufficed. "Are these his possessions?"

"Yes." She found her voice. "I gave him the watch for Christmas."

He guided her from the building and they drove her home in silence. Mayo spoke to her as they drew up once more to the flats, telling her that the following day would do very well to go through her husband's effects. "Who's your doctor? We'll get him to give you something to make you sleep tonight."

"I already have sleeping pills, thank you," she told him in a crisp, controlled voice. She appeared to have recovered her composure as completely as though she had never for a moment lost it. "And I'd prefer to carry on tonight. I've told you, I shan't be available most of tomorrow."

"It's your decision," he answered, regretting the kindly impulse that had caused him to offer to postpone the search. Certainly, it would be better from his point of view to get things moving to-night. He didn't expect it to take long, anyway.

She told them where to look when they were once more in the flat, picked up a pen and the papers she'd been reading when they rang, and let them get on with it.

There were two bedrooms, but only one was in use, a large one, with a double bed. The wardrobes were a set of mirror-faced built-in cupboards, her section of it crammed with expensive clothes and shoes, silk shirts and smart, executive-style business suits, while his contained a very few clothes which were much more casual.

"Nothing but the best, though," said Jenny Platt.

And since, apart from the clothes and some toilet things in the bathroom, there appeared to be nothing else belonging to Fleming, they returned to the living room for an examination of his papers, which were housed in a small desk in the corner of the room.

"You won't find many, though," Mrs. Fleming said. "He believed in travelling light. He kept what he was working on in his briefcase and carried it around with him."

Where was his briefcase now? It hadn't been in his car. Nor had his portable typewriter, which she also said he carried around with him. Nor had his keys. "I can't help you," she said indifferently. But the strain was telling. He fancied she was even paler than her make-up warranted; her vivid lipstick stood out like a wound. Her skin looked tight over the bones of her face.

All that was in the desk were one or two files containing copies of the articles and features he'd written and a book detailing what he had been paid for them. It was a meagre way to make a living, Mayo concluded, looking at the few items and totting up the total payments he'd received. No other source of income was apparent. His bank book tallied with his earnings. Only what had he lived on? He had dressed well, he ran an expensive car. He didn't have a joint account with his wife.

In one drawer, Kite found some handwritten notes for a feature Fleming was preparing, titled "Theatre in the Provinces."

"May I take these?" They would do well enough for the graphology experts, though the handwriting appeared to compare positively enough with the distinctive squiggles on the "suicide" note and there was no doubt in Mayo's mind that they'd been written by the same hand.

"I've no use for them," she said.

It seemed a sad epitaph for a marriage.

"What did you make of her, Martin?"

"Seen some hard-bitten females in my time, but she takes the biscuit!" Kite answered, making headway into sausage and chips in the canteen.

"You think her capable of shooting Fleming, then?" Mayo asked.

"Without turning a hair!" Kite was never lukewarm in his convictions. "But what about the note? No question the writing wasn't his, surely?"

"No, I should hardly think so. Difficult, if not impossible, to imitate, wouldn't you say? But *when* was it written—and why? Think about it: 'I've had enough. I'm packing it in. Sorry it didn't work out.' That doesn't necessarily mean he meant to kill himself. Could've been meaning to leave her, permanently, for instance. Or about anything, almost. About that job of his, maybe . . ."

"But they were all right with each other on the Sunday—according to her, at least."

"A lot of things can happen between one day and the next."

"I suppose so." Kite finished his chips and pushed his plate away. "I knew a bloke once took his wife out for their anniversary dinner and when they'd finished, he told her he was leaving her for another woman, there and then. Sent her home in a taxi, the rotten sod."

"And we wonder why women have such a low opinion of us."

"Women can be bitches too." Kite remained unshaken in his opinion. "And I reckon we've just interviewed one of 'em."

FIVE

"Mine honour is in question,
A thing till now free from suspicion."

DOWN AT HER BUTTER LANE SHOP, Lois French was carefully examining the latest finished orders of lampshades and cushions with the woman who made them up for her. There were no flaws and she'd have been extremely surprised to find any. Myra Conway was matter-of-fact, spry, middle-aged and miraculously deft with her fingers, and the articles were perfectly crafted, as they always were, no matter how unsuitable or intractable the fabrics selected by Lois's clients.

"Beautiful, Myra." Myra raised her eyes to heaven. "Well, beautifully made, anyway," Lois amended with a wry smile.

"Not everybody's choice, colours like that," Myra agreed.

They began to stack the cushions and shades on a table in the corner of the back room. Lois, whose whole life was spent harmonising colours and furnishings and creating interesting and original environments for those who could afford her prices, could hardly bear to look at the garish things. Lavenstock United had been doing particularly well this season and, as a tribute, the wife of the chairman had commissioned French Interiors to re-do her sitting room in the team's colours. Gold and a particularly virulent shade of puce, euphemistically called claret, were hardly the most felicitous choice for soft furnishings, and it seemed to Lois they'd dominated most of her waking thoughts—and some of her nightmares—for weeks. All the braids and fringes had had to be custom dyed to get that exact shade of purple-red to go with the brassy yellow of the gold, while finding a suitable fabric for the chairs to tone down all that glorious Technicolor had been next to impossible. The cost of the specially woven, quite hideous, carpet had been hair-raising. She'd seriously considered refusing the commission—after all, her reputation was at stake—until common sense prevailed. But now it was almost completed, thank God, and the client over the moon and that was nearly all that mattered.

She put coffee to brew while they discussed Myra's next batch of work, then she brought out the delicate Chinese red silk for the lampshades Myra was to cover to complement several pairs of already-finished curtains. Myra raised scandalised eyebrows while commenting on the price of the trimmings for the curtains, which had cost almost as much as the fabric itself.

"At this rate they'll have to set up a subscription fund to pay for the new stage curtains down at the Gaiety, when we we get around to doing them," she remarked.

Lois poured the coffee, Myra added sugar and milk to hers and settled for a gossip. "Terrible thing about that shooting, isn't it?"

"What shooting?" Lois picked up her own coffee cup and took a sip.

"Haven't your heard? Some poor bloke shot himself in his car up Scotley Beeches. Name of Fleming, Rupert Fleming."

The cup slid from Lois's grasp and coffee poured in a dark stream right across the Chinese silk.

"Ooh, that's done it," Myra said.

Lois seized a cloth and dabbed distractedly at the dark stain and succeeded in blotting most of it up before it spread too far. With trembling fingers, she picked up the scissors, snicked the selvedge and tore off the ruined half metre. "It could've been worse. Where . . . did you hear about this, this shooting?"

"On the late news last night, and on the radio this morning." Myra stared. "Here, you didn't know him, did you, love? Oh God, I'm sorry . . ."

"No, I didn't know him," Lois lied.

Myra looked at her shrewdly but said nothing more.

When the rest of the silk had been safely parcelled up and Myra had gone, Lois collapsed onto the nearest chair.

Rupert Fleming? She had let a demon into her life when she let him in, of that there was no question. But *suicide*?

Rupert?

Kite was still feeling peaky the next day with the aftermath of his cold, but the harder he worked the better he felt, he decided. He set himself to find out what he could about Georgina Fleming's affairs, managing to muster up a surprising amount of energy. By late afternoon, when Mayo had returned from the inquest which had, as he'd fully expected, been adjourned for further police enquiries, he was able to tell Mayo first that the shotgun's owner had been traced, and secondly that he had the information Mayo had requested about Georgina Fleming.

The shotgun was registered in the name of John Culver, residing in a house by the name of Upper Delph, adjacent to Fiveoaks Farm and not much over a mile from Scotley Beeches.

John Culver, Georgina Fleming's father.

Mayo heard the news with interest. "Long-standing feud finally resolving itself? Is that what it is?"

"Is it going to be that simple?" Kite returned.

"It usually is, isn't it?" As with most murders, its solution probably lay in the obvious, with someone in the family, some relative, or someone known to the victim being responsible. "Never neglect the obvious, laddie. It *was* his gun."

The big question in that case being what had John Culver and his estranged son-in-law been up to, meeting in Scotley Beeches at some ungodly hour of the night or morning?

"Let's go. You can tell me what you've found out about Georgina Fleming on the way."

"She runs this business with a partner, another woman," Kite informed him as they turned off the ring road and out onto the by-pass. "In fact, it's an all women affair, no men at all. It's an organisation dedicated to showing small companies how to give their businesses a vital competitive edge. One which will help them achieve aggressive growth targets and a level of excellence . . ."

"Spare me the sales patter."

Kite grinned. "Translated, it means that all these new small companies who have a good product but just don't know how to market it properly, or run the business side of their affairs, need help. That's where Georgina Fleming wheels in. It's called business consultancy."

"I know what a business consultancy is, but what qualifies Mrs. Fleming for it?"

"She took a degree in Business Studies and Administration, started out in a small way and worked her company up to what it is now. Like father, like daughter, seemingly. Nobody can keep up with her; they say she works twenty-five hours a day. One of those what they call hyperactive types, I reckon. No wonder she needs sleeping pills. No hobbies, except squash, which she plays to *win.*"

"She should play to lose?"

"No joke, even the men are terrified of her. She plays like a tiger."

Mayo, who half an hour previously had been speculating on insurances in specific relation to Georgina Fleming's late husband, said, "She's not short of a few thousand, then?"

"Ks. It's Ks, not thousands, in yuppyspeak. Serious money."

"Oh God, come off it, Martin, give it me in basic English."

"The answer's no, she isn't short. I guess she could easily have been supporting Fleming in the life to which he was accustomed and not felt a thing. But would she? I mean, they were evidently leading very nearly separate lives, weren't they? And don't forget that woman in the photo. Mrs. Fleming didn't strike me as the sort to suffer anybody being a drag on her."

"There's more ways of getting rid of a husband than blowing his head off."

"True. But whether she did it or not, I'll bet she feels it's good riddance."

"One thing I'd never bet on, Martin, and that's what Mrs. Fleming might or might not be thinking."

Grief comes in many guises. He remembered her reaction to the sight of the body. And also, that moment of softness when she'd been speaking of the Sunday evening she'd spent with her husband, and the conviction he'd had that she and Fleming had been making love. I was right about that at any rate, he thought, I was right.

Iron gates marked the beginning of Upper Delph's drive, a gravelled roadway which wound for nearly a quarter of a mile before it began to rise and they came in sight of the house.

"Stone me!" said Kite.

The ground rose even more steeply behind the house and a thick belt of trees climbed to the skyline. A hundred yards away was the old quarry, or delph, which had given the house its name, long abandoned and choked now with scrub hazel and gorse. The house had a grim and ancient appearance, a low rambling edifice with a few outbuildings straggling at the back, fronted only by a small paved garden inside a low privet hedge, with ivy scrambling to the slate roof, half-obscuring some of the windows so that it had a lowering, frowning aspect. To one side stood all that was left of a huge old conifer, its split trunk and remaining branches giving it the look of a one-armed sentinel, and at the other side a crumbling square tower, also ivy-covered, where rooks circled and cawed in the darkening afternoon.

By the time they had climbed the short flight of steps to the front door, Mayo was half-expecting to be met by the owner, armed with a shotgun. Instead, it was opened by a middle-aged woman, smartly dressed in a cherry red jersey suit that showed off a neat, well-rounded figure and complemented her plentiful dark hair and rosy cheeks. *Mrs.* Culver? Somehow, Mayo hadn't expected a wife.

He soon found, however, that she was not Culver's wife but his daily housekeeper, and that Culver himself was out, but expected back any minute. "He always takes a long walk this time in the afternoon, past the lake, but he'll be back for his tea."

Mayo said they'd wait in the car. Her eyes were bright with speculation. He could see she guessed why they were there and, taking pity on her obvious curiosity, introduced himself and produced identification.

"Come in out of the cold, why don't you? Have a cup of tea yourselves while you wait. Shouldn't be many minutes now."

Declining the tea—somehow Mayo thought it would hardly do for Culver to come back and find them sampling his hospitality before some rather stringent questions were put to him regarding his shotgun and his relations with the dead man—but accepting the offer to wait inside, Mayo and Kite followed Mrs. Stretton into a front room, where she poked up the coal fire to a bright blaze and switched on a lamp.

"Make yourselves comfortable," she said, handing Kite a newspaper before closing the door behind her.

Left to themselves, Kite looked at the paper, saw that he'd already seen it, lost interest and offered it to Mayo, but he had already begun a perambulation of the room, and declined.

There were books everywhere, on a wall of shelves and piled up untidily elsewhere. A comfortable, slightly shabby room, a sort of study or den, the furnishings a mixture of antique and the merely old, chosen for comfort and use rather than their place in some overall scheme: a wing chair that had taken its owner's shape, an upright piano with a silk runner across its top, a Georgian breakfront bookcase in the corner with a television set and a stack of records in front of it. Curtains of an undistinguished dark green rep and a carpet that had seen better days.

Culver was taking his time. A Viennese wall clock ticked the minutes away slowly and the afternoon darkened a little more while they waited. The heaped-up fire made the room very warm. Kite, who hated waiting, yawned and fidgeted at the unplanned hiatus and began idly flicking through a thick sketchbook which lay open on a small table beside where he sat, with pencils, rubbers and a box of aquarelle pastels lying beside it.

Mayo had come to a pause before a small watercolour, an amateur though not, he thought, unskilled painting of the house as it had once been, the sort of painting done by Victorian young ladies of the family. It showed the ravaged tree outside the house in all its former glory and the now ruined tower attached to a wing that had once been part of the main body of the house. He concluded there must have been a fire or some such calamity which had destroyed most of the wing, leaving only the squat remains of the tower standing. If this was the case it must have been many years since, when the Paulings owned the house perhaps, for now there was a tree growing from the centre of the tower, overtopping it by twenty feet.

"What d'you think of this?" came Kite's voice from behind him, as he held out the sketchbook.

It was nearly full, every page replete with drawings of trees, in all seasons, at every stage of growth and decay, all carefully labelled with their correct botanical name as well as their common one. Each one was, as far as either man could judge, competently drawn and subtly tinted, but more than that, there was a liveliness and vigour, a feeling for life about them that sprang from the page. Some were Arthur Rackham trees, wild and witching, others mere abstracts in their spareness and quickness of line. On one page there was a plane tree with big, maple-like leaves, the light shining on its flaking, moss-encrusted bark, making on it a diamond pattern of ruby and green. Flanking it on the next page was a group of slender silver birches with daffodils blowing beneath, under the pendulous branches. The last drawing in the book was of the crippled tree by the side of the house—*Cedrus Atlantica,* its ribbed corky bark and its one living branch investing it with a threatening air, like some ogreish wood demon.

"Wish I could draw like that!" Kite exclaimed, obviously impressed. Although he didn't know anything more about art than knowing what he didn't like, he was willing to give anyone who could hold a pencil the benefit of the doubt. "Culver, d'you think?"

"I don't know about that, but it looks like a man's work, to me."

Mayo, not much more knowledgeable than Kite, didn't know why he thought so, except that there was some strength of line about the drawings that suggested an indubitably masculine hand. But if they were Culver's, they had a sensitivity that didn't square with the hard man conjured up by that conversation with the Salisburys. Perhaps they were in for a surprise.

At that moment, they heard the man and the dog approach the house and enter by the back door. Mayo turned the pages back to where they had been left open. Not that he had too many scruples about intruding, even into something that was obviously intensely private. Scruples were something neither he nor his suspects could afford to have. But he didn't want Culver to know they'd been looking at his work.

The man's voice could be heard, evidently speaking to the housekeeper. "Still here, Molly? Whose is the car? All right, leave it ready and then you must get off." And then he was in the room with them, a tall, heavy-shouldered old man. Coarser-featured than his daughter, with a deep-clefted chin, lively dark eyes and strong bones, yet within that leathery countenance was contained a strong resemblance to Georgina Fleming. The similarity of feature was indeed quite striking, and when he spoke there was something of the same abruptness, though he was civilly polite, offering tea and, when it was refused, asking them shortly what they wanted.

The sergeant, with whom Mayo had arranged to start the questioning, began without preamble. "Do you own a double-barrelled twelve-bore shotgun, Mr. Culver?"

"I own several shotguns."

"Have you checked recently that they're all there?"

"On Sunday. Why d'you want to know?"

Kite countered with another question. "Did you know that your son-in-law, Rupert Fleming, has been found dead?"

"Yes. They said on the news he'd committed suicide." Strength and power emanated from him as he stood with his back to the fire, his dog curled at his feet. He was a harshly-spoken man, economical with words and smiles, but decisive and to the point, forceful and used to the upper hand. "Doesn't surprise me. Typical cowardly way out."

"I have to tell you the gun found by his side was traced to you."

The old man's eyes flickered, the hand holding his tobacco pouch paused. "*My* gun? How's that possible? I haven't seen him for at least seven years, nor wanted to."

"Is that so? Would you care to tell us what exactly was the trouble between you?"

Culver smiled grimly. "I've no objection. The answer is I just didn't like him. Oil and water, probably, but I also felt he wasn't good enough for my daughter—most fathers' initial reaction, I suppose. Only in his case events proved me right. As I predicted, he went from bad to worse, never amounted to anything, never would have."

"How do you account for your shotgun being in his possession?"

"I can't, I've just told you. If you're right and it is mine, I can only assume he must have stolen it, somehow. That would've appealed to his warped sense of humour, to have it traced back to me."

"Would it have been possible for it to have been taken, without your knowing?"

Culver thought about it, drawing on his pipe. "Yes, I suppose it might. I don't lock my door during the day."

"Rather unwise, sir, surely?"

"When my housekeeper's not here, I'm never far away. And anything of value I keep in the bank. If anybody wants to go to the trouble of stealing what I've got around here, they're welcome to it."

Culver's attitude was one of dry ironic detachment, as if he were humouring them, which Mayo guessed might be natural to him, but Kite was becoming wooden, in the way he did with people who rubbed him up the wrong way, and Mayo felt he'd better take over. "That's an original point of view, Mr. Culver. You feel the same way about your guns?"

"The gun room is the one place that's always kept locked."

"And the key?"

There was a short silence while Culver busied himself applying another match to his pipe, and the rich aroma of pipe tobacco was filling the room before he answered. "Ah, you can't fault me there. I keep my key with me, always."

"Just remind me again, when did you last check your guns?"

"On Sunday afternoon, like I always do."

"And not since then?"

The old man lifted his shoulders. "No need."

"What were you doing on Monday evening, Mr. Culver?"

"What I usually do. Having my supper, watching a bit of television, reading till late. I don't go to bed early these days, if I do I find myself wide awake halfway through the night."

"What time did you lock up?"

"When I went to bed—and before you ask me, I couldn't say exactly what time that was. But it's generally well after midnight when I go up."

"So you would have heard anyone trying to break in?"

"I might not, if they were quiet about it. I don't hear as well as I used to, but Minty surely would. This dog sleeps with one eye open, don't you, girl?"

They all looked at the dog on the hearthrug, apparently intent on demonstrating this phenomenon. The one open eye was amber-coloured. It reminded Mayo of Georgina Fleming's tiger eyes. He stood up. "I'd like to see where you keep your guns, please."

"You're welcome. The room's at the back."

They followed the old man along a flagged passage which ran draughtily from front to back of the house, glimpsing gloomy rooms stuffed with ancestral furniture, presumably of Pauling inheritance, until they came to a door which Culver unlocked with a key from a small bunch taken from his trouser pocket. The room was to the right of the passage, near the back door, with a window which looked onto a small, high-walled kitchen garden, beyond which the tree-covered hill rose to the skyline.

It'd be a doddle, Kite thought, getting over that wall, and if the back door was open . . . He never ceased to be amazed at folks' carelessness, and bent to examine the lock on the door. A Yale type which didn't, however, show any signs of being forced.

The room wasn't very big, probably once a pantry of some sort, flagged with the same large stones as the passage, carpeted with a worn square in the middle. On the wall opposite the windows—two small ones, neither big enough for anyone to get through—was a battered desk with a telephone, a portable typewriter and a stone jar holding pencils. To the right of the windows stood a large old-fashioned safe and on the left were the guns, tidily racked, with a shelf beneath holding cartridges and cleaning materials. Four guns, and a space where Culver said the twelve-bore should have been.

"It was there on Sunday, I know. I oiled and cleaned it with the rest and put it back." No, he said, he wouldn't necessarily have noticed if any of the guns had been missing until the next time he came to clean them. "This is the one I normally use." He indicated another twelve-bore which hung near the door. "I just unlock the door and reach out for it, or stick it back, without giving more than a glance. So used to doing it, I could put my hand on it in the dark."

"What do you keep in the safe, Mr. Culver?"

"Personal papers, a bit of loose cash."

"Would you mind checking to see if anything's missing?"

Culver raised his eyebrows but made no objection. The safe, though very large, contained nothing more than a tin cash-box and a bundle of papers which he quickly looked through and said were all present.

"And the cash-box?"

Culver unlocked it. The bit of loose cash would have amounted to a couple of thousand, possibly more, Mayo thought. "Habit of a lifetime," Culver remarked. "Can't get used to being without a bit on hand. It's all right, it's all here."

He closed and locked the box, and then the safe.

Once a scrap metal dealer, always a scrap metal dealer, Mayo thought. A roll of notes in your pocket that changed hands, no questions asked. He made a mental note that almost certainly Culver, though nominally retired, wouldn't be averse to doing a deal or two on the side now and then.

"When did you last see your daughter, Mr. Culver?" he asked, as Culver was closing the door of the little room.

The other turned to him with a smile lifting the corners of his mouth. "Yesterday afternoon, as a matter of fact," he said dryly.

"Is that so? I was given to understand there was some friction between you and Mrs. Fleming as well as with her husband?"

"*Was*, yes. Happily, that's now a thing of the past. I was seventy years old yesterday, Mr. Mayo, and Georgina came to wish me a happy birthday. We both thought it time all that was put behind us."

"Because the source of the friction had been removed?"

"Ah, but we didn't know that then, did we?"

"Didn't you, Mr. Culver? I hope that's true, for both your sakes."

Culver smiled. He said, as he opened the front door, "I'm not going to say I'm sorry he's dead, because I'm not. But you're barking up the wrong tree, if you think I'd put my own life at risk because of him."

He stood watching the policemen's car disappear down the drive. It was true that he felt not the slightest pang at the death of Rupert Fleming. Georgina was free at last, after seven years, free of Rupert Fleming, and it didn't much matter to him how this had come about.

His daughter had been born unexpectedly after several years of marriage, when he and Evelyn had long since ceased to expect children. He had felt momentarily let down when he was told that the child was not a son, one he could have moulded to his own pattern, but the disappointment had lasted only until he held her in his arms and looked into the tiny unformed mirror-image of his own face.

Evelyn's life had been sacrificed to give him the child. He deeply regretted that, though they had never been passionately in love; each had initially seen the other as a convenience, but their marriage had been amicable and when she died he had felt a sense of loss and sadness that had surprised him. They had married for practical reasons, because he had been able to provide her with the money she needed for the luxuries she thought essential to her, while she had given him, through her father, the entrée he wanted into a world where business contacts could be made through knowing the right people. They had come from different points on the social scale, though her position owed itself to her father's ability rather than his birth. He too had been a man who had made his own success, working his way diligently from counter clerk to manager of the local bank, becoming prominent in local politics and finally, for a short time before he died, at Westminster. He had always respected money and this, Culver suspected, was why there had never been any opposition to the marriage of his daughter with a man who was still, basically, a scrap metal dealer—though already, when he met Evelyn, he had been into his first half million, and the rest hadn't been long in following.

And yet, it had never been money itself that had motivated him, rather the simple need to achieve success at whatever he attempted.

If there had ever been any other passion in John Culver's life, it had been for Georgina. On her he had lavished all the love of which he was capable, though rarely showing it. Motherless, she had turned to him and they had been constant companions throughout her childhood and early adolescence. When, shortly after her return from college, she announced she was going to marry Rupert Fleming, he had been at first incredulous, then furious.

Fleming had been everything John Culver was opposed to. He had had a privileged education and thrown it away. He had had several attempts at a career and been successful at none of them. He was that unforgivable thing in John Culver's book, a dilettante, though this was not the term Culver used. His judgement was couched in much earthier terms. But Georgina, who had inherited a will as implacably averse to opposition as his own, refused to give up Fleming. Her father had spent several fruitless months while his anger mounted, trying to make her see sense, then washed his hands of the pair of them. If thine eye offends thee, pluck it out, had always been a maxim he'd lived by.

He was dimly aware that he'd done more damage to himself than to either Georgina or Fleming by this act, but he was not a man to go back on his decisions, once made. From a distance he watched her progress in the world of business with pride, grimly sticking out the loneliness, and sometimes despair, knowing that as her father's daughter she wasn't a complete fool, convinced that one day she must see the man she'd married in his true colours and come back to him.

It had taken Rupert Fleming's death for that to happen. John Culver would not have thought that too high a price for the return of his daughter.

SIX

*"Think what a torment 'tis to marry one
Whose heart is leap'd into another's bosom."*

THE POST-MORTEM RESULTS, when they came in, were straightforward enough, but for one thing.

In the report Rupert Fleming was described as a well-nourished white male, about thirty-five years of age. There were no congenital deformities, tattoo marks, old scars, or other marks of violence on the body, other than those to the head. Internal examination showed that he was in good health, that he had not eaten for some hours before he died. Death was due to cerebral lacerations caused by being shot in the head with a twelve-bore shotgun and, in the opinion of the pathologist, the wound could not have been self-inflicted. He had been dead for approximately eighteen hours when found.

The ballistics report wasn't yet available, giving an estimation of the exact distance and angles of the exit and entry wounds, nor the forensic report on the car which would amongst other things reveal the extent of any damage to it, but Timpson-Ludgate's opinion was good enough for Mayo to be going on with.

The one thing which was unexpected about the report was the presence in the body of traces of barbiturates and a considerable quantity of alcohol.

"The alcohol's understandable enough," Mayo said, "but barbiturates as well? Somebody must have slipped one to him. But I ask myself why. Why should anyone take the trouble, Martin?"

"You mean the killer needn't have bothered with the shotgun, when enough of the pills and the booze would have done the trick? It would've looked like suicide just the same . . . more so."

"The trick being, of course, to know when enough's enough. And that's it—whoever killed Fleming would have to make sure he was good and dead. Wouldn't do for him to be found before he was dead, and carted off to hospital to have his stomach pumped. As it was, the drugs would have knocked him out sufficiently for him to be moved into the driving seat before he was finished off."

"Barbiturates," Kite said. "Sleeping pills. Georgina Fleming takes sleeping pills."

"So she does."

"And it was her father's gun."

"And they cooked this up between them?"

"They could have," Kite said.

"Hm." Mayo rubbed the side of his nose with his forefinger, and thought. "That gun. I think it'd be as well to have a word with Culver's housekeeper and find out—" The telephone went. "Hold on a minute."

"Someone on the line for you, sir. She won't give her name and won't speak to anyone but you. Says she has some info on the Fleming case."

The young constable on the switchboard had been wary of passing the message direct to Mayo, rather than some lesser being, but fearful of his wrath if he didn't do so and the woman rang off, as she'd threatened. He was new and very green, but he thought she sounded nervous enough to do so. On the other hand, there'd already been the usual crop of those sure they had important information, all needing to be dealt with in case their stories happened to be true or relevant—some genuinely believing they could help, but a lot of them time-wasters, and not a few nutters. He wouldn't be thanked for wasting the D.C.I.'s time with any of those. He was relieved when Mayo told him to put her through.

"You don't know me, but my name's Bryony Harper." The soft voice came over with the hint of a West Country burr, sounding young and uncertain. "It's about . . . Rupert Fleming, that appeal you put out for anyone who's seen him recently . . ." The voice stopped, faltered.

"Take your time, Miss Harper. Presumably you have some information about where he was on Monday?"

"He was at home, here, with me and the children."

"With you?"

"Well, where else would he be? He lives here, doesn't he?"

This was the woman in the photograph. Now that the connection was made, the voice and the face seemed to fit together, like the foot in Cinderella's slipper. "Miss—Mrs.—Harper, I don't want to deal with this over the telephone. I'd like to see you."

"Yes, I expected you would, but I'm afraid you'll have to come here, I can't leave my children."

"We'll be with you as soon as possible."

The housekeeper would have to wait for the time being.

There was a sign for the Morvah Pottery on the Lavenstock Road, four miles out of Coventry, Bryony Harper had said, and here it was, a rather amateurish rendering: 'Morvah Pottery, 100 yards. Please come and look around,' with an arrow pointing the direction.

Kite manoeuvred the car down a lane so narrow that passing places had had to be constructed to allow the passage of vehicles coming from opposite directions, though they met no oncoming traffic. Nor did there seem any reason for any to be there, since there was no sign of any habitation whatsoever, not even the pottery. When they had gone for about half a mile and were just beginning to think they had missed some turning or other and Kite was muttering about the back of beyond, another sign loomed up. Welcome to Morvah Pottery, it said, and there it was, a ramshackle Victorian brick cottage with some outbuildings at the side, one of them rather grandly announcing the fact that it was the Factory Shop.

It was a bleak spot, as unwelcoming as the cold wind that sneaked round the house. As Mayo and his sergeant climbed out of the car two little boys, warmly wrapped against the cold in a random selection of woollen garments, stopped their playing in a small muddy garden mostly given over to vegetables and came to stare, in the dispassionate way of small children. When their mother came out of the doorway the elder of the little boys lost interest and ran away to clamber onto a swing suspended from the bare branches of an old apple tree. The smaller one clung to his mother's skirt and stuck his thumb in his mouth, until she bent and spoke to him, removed his thumb, wiped his nose and tucked his hair under his woollen cap.

He looked at her doubtfully for a moment, then ran off to join his brother.

The girl—she was little more—led the way into a warm, untidy kitchen, where the window was almost obscured by climbing green plants. "If you don't mind waiting a minute. I'm making bread and I can't leave it at this stage. Sorry I can't offer you a chair."

It was more of a scullery than a kitchen, unmodernised in any way, with a cracked ceramic sink and an old coal-fired range. A mound of dough was in the middle of a scrubbed deal table and she began kneading it in a gentle, haphazard sort of way that seemed part of her but didn't promise well for the finished loaves. She wasn't giving it a hard-enough time, Mayo could see, leaning against the doorpost. He remembered his grandmother making bread, punching and turning the dough energetically, leaving it in a large yellow earthenware bowl to rise, making the ancient sign of the cross in the middle, covering it with a clean tea-towel . . .

Presently she put the dough in a similar bowl and left it on a shelf above the range and then took them into a front room where the freezing cold was even more apparent after the steamy warmth of the kitchen, though she didn't seem to notice, and the furniture was Oxfam second-hand, stuff so cheerless and depressing it was hard to see how anyone could have designed, never mind bought it, in the first place. But by now Mayo felt he could hazard a guess that this was mandatory to the girl's way of life, whether she could have afforded anything else or not, a way of saying she wasn't interested in material things. She was short and plumpish and her abundant hair wasn't as dark as it had appeared in the photograph, more of a rich, glossy deep chestnut. Wide brown eyes regarded them, full of misery. She would have been pretty if her face hadn't been so blotched with crying, if she'd bothered to dress herself in something other than a long, draggle-tail black cotton skirt and T-shirt, both greyed with too frequent washing, and a big droopy cardigan which dipped at the front.

She went away and came back with coffee in thick stoneware mugs, presumably Morvah ware, and biscuits. Both were abominable, the coffee tasting as though it were made of ground acorns and the biscuits of chipboard shavings, or worse. Mayo wished he'd accepted the tea she'd offered as an alternative until she poured some for herself and he saw that it was a herb tea, red like wine, and smelling strongly of flowers.

"Mrs. Harper—"

"It's not Mrs., it's Miss, but please call me Bryony."

Bryony. Had she become what she was because of her name, a sort of self-fulfilling prophecy? Or was it the other way round—a case of adopting the name for herself to go with the life she lived? Either possibility seemed likely; she was a left-over flower child, too young to have been of that generation, but surely a spiritual descendant.

"He really is dead?" she whispered. Tears welled up again, large and heavy. "Oh, I'm so stupid, of course he is—only, I can hardly believe it. What made him do . . . what he did? After living with him for nearly two years, that's the one thing I'd have sworn he'd never do."

"Two years?"

She'd caught his swift, involuntary glance outside, to where the children were chasing round, shouting and laughing now, their cheeks rosy with the cold air. "No, the boys aren't his. He didn't want babies, not yet. Their father . . . I had this relationship with someone, you see, we started the pottery together. I was lucky he didn't want his share back when he left," she finished simply.

How much would his share have amounted to? Not enough for him, whoever he'd been, this potter, to have given a second thought to leaving it behind when he departed, it seemed. Barely enough, one would have thought, to support the girl and her two children. Mayo said gently, "Can we begin by establishing the last time you saw Mr. Fleming?"

"It was about half past seven on Monday when he left. He had to get over to Lavenstock to meet someone."

"Did he say who?" She shook her head. "Or what it was about?"

"No, I just supposed he was covering some sort of story, though he did seem excited about it. He said he'd be back as soon as he could make it."

"Did he often spend days away like that?"

"If he had a story to follow up. But he never spent more time away than he had to. He used to say he could relax here with me and recharge his batteries."

She went to pull aside the window curtain, ostensibly to check on the children in the garden, but really to make use of a wad of tissue pulled from her pocket. Presently she came back, nervously plucking off the leaf of a tradescantia that tumbled from a shelf above the table while contemplating her feet, shod in flat black lace-ups with thick crepe soles, worn with black woollen stockings. There was a smear of flour on her cheek. "You know he was married?" she asked suddenly in a choked voice, looking up and flushing. "Yes, well . . . he hasn't seen her for years, but she wouldn't divorce him, you know, she's a strong Catholic. Not that marriage would have made any difference to us, we didn't need to make any public vows to prove our commitment."

Her naivety was so simple it was nearly unbelievable. Her gaze travelled from one to the other, her eyes beseeching them to believe her, as if this might allow her to believe Fleming's lies too. She must have known there was nothing to stop Fleming divorcing Georgina if they'd been separated for years, as he said, regardless of either Georgina's wishes or her religious beliefs, real or invented. Fleming had spun Bryony a tale, just as he'd spun Georgina one. And neither woman had believed him, though both had pretended to, for their own reasons—so what had it been about Rupert Fleming, apart from his arrogant, haughty good looks, that had made his women go along with the doubtful game he played and sorrow for him when he was dead?

"I once saw her, you know. I got someone to look after the children for the afternoon and I got a bus into Lavenstock. I went to that place where she works, where she has her business, and I saw her." She didn't seem to realize she had just sadly, pathetically confirmed what he suspected. She hugged her arms across her chest as if the cold of the room had at last got to her and said without a trace of envy, yet looking very young and vulnerable, "She's very—good-looking, isn't she? And very power—" She hesitated, fumbling for the right word but not finding it. "Well, anyway, that's just what he couldn't stand about her. Her being so pushy and so unfeminine, the way she made everyone else feel such a fool, it was everything he despised."

So much so, thought Mayo sardonically, that he had returned from this rural slumming when it suited him to that smartly-furnished flat, his stylish wife and his expensive suede jackets. Whatever his feelings for Bryony Harper, they hadn't stood up to sharing her lifestyle permanently, though it seemed to have suited him to put up with the simple poverty of this life for short periods of time. Perhaps because she was everything his wife was not: pliable, warm, loving, undemanding . . . but demonstrably unlike his wife in that she was not well off. If he had left Georgina and gone to live permanently with Bryony, how would they have lived? His own earnings hadn't amounted to a row of beans. He wondered what Bryony had made of the Porsche, the suede jacket, the Rolex.

And so Fleming had had the best of both worlds, and divided his life between them.

"To die like that after all the care he took of himself!" She was weeping unashamedly again, unable to stop the flow of tears. At last she abandoned herself totally to the flood, mopping up with the soggy tissues. He waited patiently until it had abated before asking her what she'd meant.

"Just that he was always so fussy about himself," she sniffed. "Nothing but wholefood, organic vegetables, things like that. He hardly ever drank—well, not often—and he had a very strict exercise programme. He wasn't a hypochondriac, don't think that, but he'd never do anything to injure his health. He so hated the thought of being ill—and *dying*, well! . . . he was terrified of it, really."

He said, "Bryony, did you know any of his friends or his associates?"

As he'd expected, she shook her head, but then she said, "Oh, he did mention once the people connected with that theatre in Lavenstock, what's it called, the Gaiety? He used to do reports on their productions for the local papers. I think he was writing a feature on it as well, something like that, but I don't remember any names."

"Did he ever mention anyone, however casually, who had reason to dislike him?"

"I knew hardly anything about his life outside these four walls.

But he wouldn't have killed himself just because someone didn't like him, would he? Oh goodness, what are you saying? Are you saying he *didn't* kill himself?"

He could tell her now. It would soon be public knowledge, anyway. "I'm afraid that's what it looks like."

But his cautious answer, rather than distressing her further, seemed to calm her in some strange way. "Poor Rupert," she said, sounding suddenly vastly older and more experienced. "But I'm so *thankful* he didn't have any reason to take his own life." She lapsed into silence. The voices of the children outside were raised in an excited game. "But he wasn't really happy, you know. He had such a lot of anger in him. He said I was helping him to learn to let it go and I think I was."

"Anger? What about?"

"The unfairness of everything, the way things never seemed to go right for him, not for long." She shook her head. "I don't know, it was all tightly locked up inside him, he could be so secretive. It made him hard and distrustful sometimes, too, but he couldn't help himself. He was good to me—and he loved the children." Her voice caught on another sob. "What am I going to do?" she ended desolately.

Mayo felt exceedingly sorry for the hopelessness of her situation, but at the same time he wanted to tell her to shake herself and get out into the real world, and knew it would do no good, she would take no notice. She was naive and incurably romantic, she would always be at the mercy of her emotions; there'd be another potter, another Rupert Fleming, in time. Life, he was afraid, would always do this to the Bryony Harpers of this world.

"Is there no one who can help you?"

"Only my mother, and she doesn't approve of—of the way I like to live my life, and everything."

"Perhaps you could get her to come and stay with you for a while, all the same."

"Oh, no! Although maybe she would come, now."

He stood up. "In the circumstances, I'd appreciate it if you'd let myself and Sergeant Kite take a look at Mr. Fleming's belongings."

"You're welcome, but you won't find anything. He believed in travelling light."

"What about his writing things—his typewriter and his briefcase?"

"No, not even that. He always carried them with him."

But neither had been in his car, Mayo reflected, as they sifted through the few things he had kept at the cottage. They found nothing except items of clothing, a few books which charted the unsteady progress of his life . . . handbooks on photography, insurance selling, and, concealed under some sweaters, one or two magazines which he felt sure Bryony didn't know about, and of which Kite took charge.

"Would you like to see the pottery?" Bryony asked as they were leaving. Mayo had no desire to, the thought of it depressed him, but Kite, giving the girl his nicest smile, surprised him by announcing that he certainly would. Mayo knew what it would be like and was in no way surprised. The usual kiln and a couple of wheels and a few shelves on the back wall displaying the wares for sale. Competently thrown, but unoriginal and decorated in the usual drab shades of earth. Though he couldn't imagine what he was going to do with them, he bought a couple of mugs and a small bowl, and Kite bought a thing like a cremation urn that she said was a *pot-pourri* container.

They drove off and Kite said, "Would you credit it? Two homes, two women. Some blokes have it made."

"Nice turn of phrase you have, Martin."

Kite intercepted the look flashed at him and paused to think about what he'd said. "Sorry. I should be more careful how I choose my words, shouldn't I? What I should've said was, 'Some women seem to cop for everything and Fleming was a bastard who had it coming to him, one way or another.'"

"Better. I reckon that about sums it up, in fact."

They drove in silence for some time until Kite said, "We assumed, didn't we, that Fleming was given the barbiturates in the alcohol. Which is funny because she—Bryony—just said he didn't drink much . . ."

"Everybody breaks their own rules occasionally, especially in times of stress," Mayo answered absently, glancing at his watch as they reached the main road and the Morvah Pottery was left behind. "Talking of which, let's see if we can find somewhere for lunch. I need something to take the taste of Bryony Harper's coffee away."

"Unbelievable, wasn't it? It's an art, knowing how to make coffee as bad as that. But the biscuits were worse." Kite thought a moment and then said he knew a pub they could go to. "Nice little place called the Woodman, they have smashing Cornish pasties, home-cooked and not all potato like some."

"I'll accept your word as a connoisseur. What about the beer?"

"That's not bad, either. It'll mean a detour, but not more than a mile or two, and it's worth it."

In a few minutes, Kite turned off the main road into a lesser one and the car began to climb. The landscape here was of rolling hills, where the soil was red and friable, and wide agricultural vistas spread to either side. As they reached the summit of the hill Mayo, having orientated himself, said, "Pull in when you can, will you? That's Scotley Beeches down there, and I'd like to take a look. We should get a bird's-eye view from up here."

Having found a gateway a few yards ahead, Kite drew in to the side, off the road. They left the car and stood looking over the forest, extensively spread below them, gradually thinning as it climbed the folds of the hills rising opposite from the valley bottom. Down below, the orderly buildings and the manor house that comprised Fiveoaks Farm lay to the left, with a tractor and a Range Rover parked outside one of the barns. A footpath emerged from the forest, crossing the valley behind the farm and coming out onto the Lavenstock Road by way of a small coppice. Upper Delph could be seen, sitting at right angles, with its ridge of trees rising behind it and its long drive winding down to meet the main road. From here, too, could be seen something that was hidden from anyone arriving via the drive—the extent of the abandoned quarry, the little lake with its skiff moored at the edge, and the daffodils under the birches.

As they watched, Culver came out of the house with the brown and white dog at his heels. They saw him walk across to one of the outbuildings and open the door. Presently, a large Volvo Estate was reversed out, the door opened for the dog to jump in, and Culver drove off.

"I think that gives us our cue to go and see Mrs. Stretton," Mayo said. "Come on."

"Hey, what about my cornish pasties? I haven't eaten since breakfast and I was just working up to them."

"They'll keep. We shouldn't be all that long, anyway, and I'd like to see Mrs. Stretton alone."

She answered the door with a pair of rubber gloves in her hands, suds still clinging to them. "I'm sorry, you've just missed Mr. Culver."

"It's you we wanted to see, Mrs. Stretton."

Her eyes widened. "Excuse me, I was just finishing the washing up. Come in to the kitchen, will you?"

They followed her along the wide, through passage to the kitchen at the back of the house. Like the gun room opposite, it had windows facing the back premises and the woods which rose behind the house. It was an enormous kitchen by modern standards, Kite reckoned two and a half times the size of his own at least, heated by the big Aga found in most country kitchens and still warmly redolent of pastry and roasted meat, sharply reminding him of the hollow in his stomach. Despite its size, it was comfortable and homely and equipped with all the gadgets nowadays considered necessary to maintain life, from a washing machine down to a dishwasher, though Mrs. Stretton, evidently one of the old school, had been washing up out by hand.

She picked up a drying-up cloth and continued working as she spoke to them, having first provided them with cups of tea. Mayo sometimes thought he could die of tannin poisoning, the amount of tea he'd drunk in the course of his professional life. She told them she'd left the house on the previous Monday at half past four sharp, as she always did, because her husband met her with his car at the main gate, unless it was very bad weather, in which case he'd drive up to the house. "He's semi-retired, see, with just a little part-time job. Keeps you in trim, having something to do besides watching the flowers on the wallpaper grow. Same reason I've stayed on here as long as I have. I've been here a long time and I enjoy it. Mr. Culver's easy enough to work for . . . he has his funny ways, I don't deny, but I speak my mind and he does the same and it seems to work. I come at eleven, cook him his main meal so he doesn't have to bother with anything much at night and then see to whatever's to be done in the house. He takes the dog out every afternoon, regular as clockwork, and I leave his tea ready and if he isn't back by half past four I just go."

"Leaving the door open."

She pursed her lips. "We won't say too much about that! I keep telling him there's some real funny folk about nowadays but he won't listen. Doesn't want to be bothered thinking about taking his keys with him every time he goes out, he says. Maybe he'll listen to me a bit more now, though how anybody got into the gun room without breaking the door down, I don't know, because he always keeps that key with him."

Polishing the last plate and putting it away with the rest, she rinsed her hands, hung her drying cloth over the rail above the Aga and came to join them at the table.

"Anything else you remember about last Monday, Mrs. Stretton?"

"Nothing special about Monday," she answered, rubbing rose-scented hand cream carefully into her hands, "but Tuesday, yes. It was his seventieth birthday, you know. Never said a word to me, mind, or I'd have got him a bit of a present and a card, cooked him something special. It's not every day you're seventy, is it? I wouldn't have known at all, if it hadn't been for Georgina coming. And about time, too, and so I told her. First time she'd set foot here since she married that chap of hers. I used to tell her it wasn't right, but she never did listen to any advice, any more than her father does."

"It sounds as though you knew Mrs. Fleming before she married."

"Bless you, of course I did! Long before. I came here when she was a little girl, no more than eleven or twelve she'd be. And what's more, I've kept in touch with her since she left. I don't hold with all this bickering between families and whatnot, life's too short and so I used to tell her. But they're too much alike, those two, needed their heads banged together if you ask me. You'd never credit it—Georgina ringing me up and asking me how her father was, making me swear not to tell him . . . and him pretending he didn't want to know when I let fall a few snippets about her—but with his ears flapping all the time like a donkey's! Stupid, it was, don't you think?"

They agreed that it was, then Mayo asked what time Mrs. Fleming had come to the house on Tuesday and was told it had been just as Mrs. Stretton was leaving.

"Half past four?"

"Or thereabouts."

"I see. When are you expecting Mr. Culver back, Mrs. Stretton?"

"I couldn't say. Said he'd a bit of business to attend to, but he'd be back before I left, that's all I know."

"All right then, we'll leave you to get on with your work, but I'd like to take a look at the wood behind the house before we go. No need to bother yourself, we'll go out of the back door here and see ourselves off when we've finished. Can you get out onto the main road down through the wood?"

"Oh, you can get through, I daresay, but it'll be a rough old struggle, and muddy. There's no proper path till you get down into the valley, and it's a fair walk right round and back up the drive."

"That's all right, we keep boots in the back of the car, and the sergeant here enjoys a good walk."

"Bloody hell," muttered Kite as they went out into the courtyard at the back and climbed the wall into the wood, seeing the prospects of his lunch fading into suppertime.

There was a path of sorts, but so choked and overgrown with what seemed like an impenetrable barrier of brambles, thorns and long trails of ground ivy that they might never have found it had they not been carefully looking for it. Mayo plunged into it, pushing vegetation aside with scant regard for his clothing. A pheasant started in front of them. Startled wood pigeons clattered away overhead. Kite reluctantly followed, cursing as he dodged the spiteful backlash of the bramble tentacles Mayo had pushed aside. Pausing to suck a bleeding scratch on the back of his hand, he saw daylight ahead, and a few paces more brought him level with Mayo, who was standing at the edge of this little wood, looking down at the barely discernible footpath that led down and behind Fiveoaks Farm and ended in the little coppice by the roadside.

"This is the way he came, whoever pinched the gun," he said.

"Nothing easier. All he had to do was to come up here, hide himself in the woods and watch for his opportunity and just walk into the house, between Mrs. Stretton leaving and Culver coming back in."

"*If* he pinched it. If it wasn't Culver himself who killed Fleming. And it doesn't explain, either," said Kite, breathing heavily, "how he got into the gun room."

"Nor does it," Mayo agreed. "But look, that footpath down there, the one which runs behind the farm, is in direct line from the spot in the forest where the Porsche was." He was frowning as he spoke, thinking things out. "Anybody who knows the area, or who'd sussed it out, would've known about it. What's the betting there was a car hidden behind the coppice ready for a smart getaway? I want somebody to take a careful look at it."

"I think you're right. I'll have it seen to," Kite promised.

"Come on then, let's get back."

"Back? The way we came?"

"Unless you want to miss your lunch. It'll take at least three quarters of an hour to walk all the way down into the valley and back up by the drive. We might just get to the Woodman before they close if we hurry."

SEVEN

"This dangerous bridge of blood! Here we are lost."

THE FIRST THING Alex noticed was that the window displays of Lois's shop had been changed since she last called. The one facing onto the Cornmarket was now set out as an elegant study, exhibiting dark rich fabrics and masculine wallpapers, and the other, round the corner in Butter Lane, had been arranged to show off a display of Chinese art: pictures which were merely a few delicate brushstrokes, different-coloured jade carvings and porcelain in lighted niches, with a yellow-washed silk carpet dominating the display. She stood looking at the windows for some time before going in, admiring her sister's flair, as others must, since Lois was so far from being short of commissions that she was looking for a sympathetic partner. Proving, she said, that one didn't need to be in the King's Road to make an impression.

"Sorry I haven't been around," Alex apologized as she closed the door behind her. "The whole strength's been up to the ears with this Fleming case, and you were out the one evening I called."

"Darling," Lois answered, flicking rapidly through a new sample wallpaper book which had just arrived, "just because we live in the same town doesn't mean we have to be in each other's pockets all the time. Sometimes I think it's a mistake to live too near one's family."

Alex, who wasn't normally a touchy sort of person, felt bereft of speech for a moment. Whose fault was it they lived so close to each other? Had Lois conveniently forgotten that she was the one who had pressed Alex to have herself transferred to Lavenstock in an effort to start a new life, to put her disastrous affair with her married Irish lover behind her? Who had reminded her that Gil Mayo, an old friend whose wife had recently died, had also made the switch from the north of England? Advice that Alex had acted upon—thereby setting up a whole new set of problems for herself, and incidentally for Gil too, though this wasn't the time to brood on that.

Anyway, to say they lived in each other's pockets when they saw each other at most a couple of times a week was one of Lois's outrageous exaggerations and best ignored.

She took a deep steadying breath. "How's the production going?"

"Frankly, I'm beginning to wish I'd never got myself involved."

"I thought you were enjoying it."

"I *was.*"

"What's gone wrong?"

Lois shrugged, without replying. Oh Lord, Alex thought, what now? The Lavenstock Thespians were an amateur group whose status had risen considerably over the last couple of years, ever since the appointment by the Town Council of an ex-actor called Ashleigh Cockayne who was known as a Community Drama Director, an umbrella title that covered drama in schools, theatre workshops and the running of a community centre in the town. Since his appointment the Thespians had won several awards in dramatic festivals up and down the country and now played to nearly full audiences whenever they staged a production. Lois had become involved initially through agreeing to supply certain props for their current production, and then by helping with the sets.

The unaccountable waning of her original enthusiasm seemed part and parcel of everything else that was the matter with her at the moment, Alex thought, sighing inwardly. There was a new petulance in her tone as she wandered around, rearranging things unnecessarily, and the amused irony with which she regarded herself and life in general seemed to have completely disappeared. Lois happy was a joy to all, but Lois miserable was glum indeed. "It was interesting at first," she admitted after a few moments, "but the last two rehearsals have been such an utter *shambles,* all they can talk about now is that—that man who was supposed to have shot himself. But now it's murder, isn't it?"

Her back to Alex, she stood in front of a mirror at the end of the shop. Alex could see her reflection, poised and guarded. She was as immaculately turned out as ever, but the smart polished ebony of her short new haircut went hard with her small, piquant pale face.

Her eyes, looking for Alex's reaction, were watchful and wary and Alex noticed new small lines that had appeared round the corners of her mouth. Then all of a sudden she understood what Lois was saying, what had been going on these last few weeks. Two and two came smartly together and her irritation with her sister began to disperse.

"I've been a fool," she said quietly. "I should've guessed. I'm sorry, Lois."

"How could you have guessed?" Lois turned and faced her and didn't bother to pretend that she didn't understand Alex. "And I'm the one who's been the fool. I knew the whole thing was a disaster from the start but I couldn't stop myself." Her lips twisted. "At my age you'd think I'd have learned more sense."

"I suppose we shall all still be saying that when we're ninety."

Alex wanted to reach out and draw her sister to her and tell her to have a good cry, but years of helping Lois over the various crises in her life had taught her better. "What you need's a stiff drink," she announced briskly, in her best police sergeant manner.

"Darling, any more and you'll be bringing out your little breathalyser! What I'd really like's a good cup of hot tea." She looked at her watch, which said twenty minutes to closing time, then walked over to the door and turned the Open sign to Closed. "What the hell. Come on upstairs."

She was changing the room round *again*, Alex saw as they entered the flat's sitting room. A sure sign she was unsettled. Instead of the fashionable country house clutter which had been her current obsession, the room looked bare, as if being stripped for action. What would it be this time? Art Deco? Or back-to-medievalism Arts and Crafts? Probably the Oriental Look, if the Butter Lane window was anything to go by, but what a shame, Alex thought, to get rid of all that pretty knick-knackery, the little French clock Gil admired so much, the gold-framed watercolours and the charming collection of old scent bottles, snuff boxes and the like, all the small, valuable antiques that Lois, with her nose for a bargain, had picked up over the years.

Ten minutes later, when they were drinking fragrant smoky Lapsang Souchong from thin porcelain cups and Lois was leaning back looking a little more relaxed, she said abruptly, "I suppose, having told you so much, you've a right to know the rest."

Alex studied the shadowy outline of the cup's pattern which showed through on the inside like blue veins under white skin. There was something to be said for Lois's contention that good tea tasted better from delicate porcelain, and strong, milky breakfast coffee from a huge, dark green Continental cup. Gil found attitudes like this precious, but perhaps the thick white all-purpose cups they used down at the station did account for the all-purpose taste of any liquid poured into them. She looked at Lois and said, "Not if you don't want to tell me. And as long as you understand that I can't keep anything that's relevant to myself."

"There isn't anything relevant as you call it, my love, not really. I scarcely knew the first thing about Rupert Fleming, if you want the truth, unless you count knowing that he was selfish and egotistical to a degree I've rarely met in anyone before. He really was a cold-hearted devil, though he could be charming when he wanted—God, couldn't he just!—but it was all a big act. Oddly enough, he couldn't act at all on stage. They tried him in several parts but he was a complete fiasco. I've sometimes thought it was as if he was permanently acting a part in real life and felt if he let himself go on stage he'd reveal the real Rupert."

"What a horror you make him sound! And yet—?" Alex stopped, not quite knowing how to put it.

"And yet we had this thing going for us, is that what you're trying to say? Well, chemistry, what else? Sheer animal magnetism, and I'm not over it yet, though given a few more weeks and I would've been, I daresay. I really didn't like him very much, you know. To be honest—he frightened me sometimes. And I frightened myself because I couldn't tell him to keep away. My God, I've never thought I was one of *those* women . . ."

"What do you mean, he frightened you?"

"I don't know." Lois looked deep into her cup, as if the answer lay there. "I felt as though I'd never really know him, that no one would. I couldn't understand why he hung around the theatre, for instance . . ."

"That was where you met him?"

"Yes. There didn't seem to be anything in it for him. He couldn't act, as I've said, and he wasn't involved in the production in any other way. And he definitely wasn't the sort to waste himself. Then I began to wonder if he and our dear Arts Director weren't up to something."

"Cockayne?"

"Ashleigh Cockayne, if you can believe a name like that. Just designed for a Sir in the next Honours list, isn't it? Too bad he'll never make it," she said acidly, adding, too hastily for Alex's liking, as though she regretted having gone so far but realized she couldn't fairly back down at this point. "Don't ask me what was going on, I haven't a clue . . . but they were down there together all hours, and there was something unspoken running between them. I can't explain it better than that. It was simply a feeling I had."

"Did you speak to anyone about this?"

"Theatre people, even amateurs, aren't the sort who ever actually listen when you want to talk. They're too wrapped up in themselves and too conscious of the impression they're making. But someone mentioned it to *me*—that nice young policewoman of yours, Janet Lindsay. She hinted—oh, very discreetly—that she'd wondered too."

"Janet? Good heavens, I didn't realize Janet fancied herself as an actress! Really?"

Alex tried to visualise the calm, matter-of-fact young Scottish W.P.C. with her smoothly pinned-up fair hair giving her all to a part in a Renaissance tragedy, and failed.

"She doesn't act. She helps behind the scenes and prompts, that sort of thing. They call her the Assistant Stage Manager on the programmes, which means general dogsbody, but she seems to enjoy it."

"And?"

"What do you mean, and?"

"And what else?"

"There *is* nothing else. What else should there be, for God's sake?"

"I don't know," Alex said. But she *did* know her sister, and wondered.

If, for instance, Lois had yet gone beyond the shock of hearing of Rupert's death and its effect on her emotionally and come to the realization of what her connection with the dead man might really mean to the police.

The next morning W.P.C. Janet Lindsay woke up feeling rather put out, unusual for her. Her natural inclination and her police training combined to make her normally calm and unruffled at all times. Most times. But really, she did think Mitch might have met her at the airport.

She hoped he wasn't sulking because she'd resolutely refused to cancel her pre-arranged holiday in Rhodes with Kate and go skiing with him, though sulkiness had never been part of Andrew Mitchell's make-up . . . and she'd been so certain that she'd succeeded in getting him round to her way of thinking. He'd agreed that of course she couldn't let Kate down, miserable as she was after that rotten divorce . . . after all, he and Janet hadn't even been going out together when the holiday with Kate had been arranged, months ago. He'd eventually settled, cheerfully enough she'd thought, on spending the first week of his leave near Klosters, on his own. Only she wasn't to blame him, he said, if he found some local talent to share his holiday with him.

That was a joke. He was a great one for jokes, Mitch. No one, not even Janet, ever called him Andrew, or even Andy, though it was sometimes Einstein down at the station, on account of having his nose in a book whenever he could. His good humour made him very popular with everyone and he could take as good as he gave, never taking offence. He and Janet hadn't known each other all that long, only since she'd joined the force six months ago, but they'd spent most of their time together since then, while agreeing to keep their own interests as well. She had the Thespians and Mitch had his reading to keep up with . . . he was hoping to be accepted as an external university student and read for a Law Degree. He was very ambitious. He wasn't going to stay on a constable's pay any longer than he could help.

Janet, with true Scottish caution, kept telling herself that she hadn't yet decided whether or not to be serious about him. But she smiled whenever she thought of him and something inside her made her blood do a little dance. And a future which didn't include Mitch seemed too dismal a thing to contemplate. Rhodes hadn't been much fun without him and she could hardly bear all the delays and frustrations of the journey home, hour after boring hour before departure.

And then, when she'd rung him as arranged, so that he could pick her and Kate up, there was no answer. She'd assumed some emergency which had called him in off leave, especially when there was still no reply this morning.

She didn't want to ring in to the station to find out what had happened, because with a slightly sinking feeling she asked herself if it was just possible that he *had* found someone else to share his holiday, and stayed on. But how stupid can you get, she thought, chiding herself and deciding that with his usual impetuosity he *had* stayed on, but simply because he was enjoying himself. There'd be a postcard tomorrow.

But the slightly depressed feeling wouldn't go away, so she decided she might as well make the best of it and go down to the Gaiety for the Saturday morning rehearsal that had been called for that day.

"There's something I think you should know, sir, about the Fleming case," Alex said, looking up from the charge sheets she was sorting through in the front office as Mayo and Kite came in.

"Right, come up to my office, would you, Sergeant? We were just going to have some coffee there. Organise another cup, will you, Kite?"

Kite winked at the desk sergeant at all this formality as he went off to perform his office-boy duties. There was scarcely anyone at the station who wasn't aware by now of the association which existed between the extremely attractive Sergeant Jones and the Chief Inspector. It wasn't the sort of thing you could keep secret for long in Lavenstock, especially not in a police station. But no one made jokes about it. That wouldn't have gone down well at all with Mayo who, Kite was sure, was well aware of the gossip, but who kept his private life very largely to himself. Nor, Kite suspected, with Alex Jones either. He could imagine the fire flashing from those dark blue eyes if anyone had dared to make any snide remarks or innuendoes.

Upstairs, when Kite eventually brought in the coffee, the atmosphere soon slipped into a more friendly mode. After all, he and Alex were of equal rank, and Mayo was never one to stand on his dignity. "I suppose you want your usual disgusting amount of sugar, Martin?" she asked, handing him his cup, not leaving him to pour out his own as more and more of the female strength, even the youngest, were inclined to do.

"Only two and a half. I'm trying to cut down." Kite had an insatiable sweet tooth and the campaign against sugar was bad news for him.

Mayo watched Alex as she poured, bending over the table, her movements graceful even at such a mundane task, and realized just how much he'd give to be able to spend one of those long, lazy evenings together which they quite often managed, despite the constraints of their jobs. They could eat something special which they both liked. He had a new record, Barenboim conducting Beethoven's Ninth, and afterwards, they'd make love, and it would be marvellous and he would wonder why the hell Alex wouldn't agree to their getting married so that it could be like this all the time. And then he'd start wondering whether she was, after all, right in her decision to live apart—whether it wasn't better to be together when they chose, rather than have custom stale the infinite variety et cetera, et cetera.

He finished his coffee and with difficulty brought his mind to bear on what Alex was saying. She was talking about her sister and as the tale unfolded he began to realize he'd have to climb down and admit that this time she'd been right to be worried about Lois. He marvelled again at the intuition between the two women. He could never make out whether this was normal between sisters or some other exceptional facet of Alex's character.

She came rather self-consciously to a halt. She'd had to tell them of the affair between Lois and Rupert Fleming, but she'd glossed over it as much as she felt she could. She saw the glance which passed between the two men and knew she hadn't fooled either of them.

Lois, yet another of Fleming's women! Mayo was thinking. Regular Casanova he'd been and no mistake. "What sort of thing did she suspect was going on between Fleming and Cockayne, then?" he asked.

Alex thought about the evasion that had crept into Lois's story at that point. "I'm not sure she knows . . . or wants to admit," she said carefully. "Their relationship—Lois and Rupert's, I mean—well, she's very much on edge and awfully touchy about it. You see, she didn't really *like* him very much and if she admits what she really thinks and it shows him in an even worse light, she'll despise herself even more for being attracted to him."

This feminine logic was beyond Kite, for one. He looked baffled and said rather shortly, "Despising herself might be the least of her worries, doesn't she realize that? The man's been murdered, Alex, and he was her lover."

He thought he might have gone too far when he saw the expression on her face. She averted her dark, sleek head to gaze out of the window for a moment, but then said calmly, "I've thought of that, of course. She's not such a fool that she'll try to hide anything, but I didn't want to press her at that moment. I think she's relieved she's got it off her chest and she'll be able to talk about it soon enough."

"As long as she doesn't take too long," Mayo said shortly, making a mental note to see that she didn't. "Meanwhile, I'd like to talk to Lindsay, see what her impressions were."

"I'm afraid she's on leave until Monday. I think she's in Crete. No, it was Rhodes."

"Doesn't matter if it's Timbuctoo if she isn't here. We'll have to go down to the Gaiety without the benefit of seeing her, then. This isn't the first time we've had that place mentioned in connection with Fleming."

Georgina Fleming entered the garden in Folgate Street through a pair of tall, wrought-iron gates set in a wall of ancient brick, part of the original fabric of a long-demolished Cistercian foundation.

Inside the gates, it was like being in church, an enclosed oasis of peace in the busy town, the traffic noise muted by the high walls. They would be entirely private here. Walkers of dogs weren't allowed in the garden and mothers with prams and children preferred the Rec with its swings and slides, thank God. It was too cold and too early in the year as yet for the elderly to sit and doze on the seats in the sun and enjoy the aromatic scents breathed out into the air; the wrought-iron gates, kept shut to deter stray animals, also intimidated the casual passer-by, though in fact they were only locked at sundown. It suited her purpose that the garden and its botanical treasures, though open and free to all, wasn't better used. But the charm of its rare plants and box-edged parterres was elusive; most people didn't care for a garden where there were no bedding-out schemes or herbaceous borders.

It hadn't been Rupert's scene either. She'd brought him here at that early point in their acquaintance when she had wanted them to know everything about each other, to share delights. But he'd rushed her through the garden like the Red Queen. Faster, faster.

Don't think of it. Don't.

Georgina would've liked to have had a garden, was knowledgeable about the theory of it, as she was about so much. She picked up knowledge as a magnet picks up iron filings, and she had a keen eye for the rightness of things. She would've loved to dig and mow and energetically rake up leaves in autumn, and plan grandiose schemes . . . but it was no good, she'd never make a true gardener. She knew only too well that she lacked any kind of patience. Inactivity she couldn't bear at any time. And just now it was insupportable.

Pigeons lumbered away from her rapid impatient strides ringing on the stone-flagged paths as she increased her pace, though the starlings, bold as ever, continued to strut around in an opportunist way, hoping for crumbs. The old bricks of the walls were a tapestry of purple and cream and rose, the length of one making a setting for half a dozen seventeenth-century bee-boles, set into it at intervals. And here in the middle of the wall was the bronze plaque, green with age, that her father had first shown her, announcing that the garden was dedicated to William Corbyn who had begun and endowed it, he who had scoured the world to bring back the strangeness and beauty of exotic plants from remote places.

How that would be frowned upon nowadays, plundering other nations' stores of riches—all the same, she was on the side of William Corbyn and all the others of his ilk. Think of it, no Kew, no Chelsea Physic Garden, no azaleas, or even crocus . . .

"Hello, George."

No one, but no one, had ever been allowed to call her that except Tim. And he'd long since forfeited that right. She turned and stared at him, tweed-capped and Barbour-jacketed, coldly.

"What is it you want?" she asked shortly, looking at her watch. She would give him ten minutes, no more. She'd already lost more than enough time recently. She was very much afraid Tim Salisbury might be going to turn into a nuisance, and his first words confirmed the fear.

"Well," he said, "he's gone, now."

She wondered how she could ever have thought she loved him, or even liked him, this pompous, self-satisfied *dull* man, how she could have contemplated marrying him and becoming a county farmer's wife. There would have been compensations, of course. It would have pleased her father, for one thing, because there would have been plenty of money. And position, if that was what mattered to you. Time on one's hands, all the time in the world, which was never a thing Georgina wanted. She would have found occupations, of course she would. But there would have been nothing for her mind to do. No excitement for her body.

Salisbury watched her face, palely made-up and with the sort of bright, deep-coloured lipstick he associated with his mother and other women when he was a child, her nails painted to match—even that frightful hair-do. It was the in thing, he supposed vaguely, and awful as he thought it, it somehow looked right on her, part of the whole. She'd always had style, it was in everything about her—her fashionable clothes, the boots, the slim, boyish, almost breastless figure . . . he felt a sudden surge of long-buried desire, as strong as any he had ever felt for her. He reached out for her hand.

But the movement turned into an ungainly grab and she managed to outmanoeuvre him, disconcerting him as she'd always done, even when they'd been children and, later, lovers, by asking, "How is Susan?"

The last person he wanted to be reminded of at this moment was Susan. Susan was something apart, rarefied, different from other women, nothing at all to do with this old remembered longing he felt just now for Georgina. It was a desecration to talk of her in such a context. "Let's leave her out of this, shall we?"

"Isn't it too late for that—a long way too late?" She found him, after all.

He knew she was right, and this and the small mocking smile with which she said it made him brutal. "Don't start pretending at this stage that you were happy with him," he said, and had his small revenge when he saw how he'd succeeded in needling her, but it didn't last long. Her eyes, those curious tigress eyes, were like a liquid-gold fire that reduced him to jelly, and he knew with a sick feeling that Fleming was still part of her dream, in that secret place where he, Tim, never had been and never would be admitted.

"What do you know about my happiness?" she demanded, the last syllable drawn out so that it was nearly a hiss.

"Enough to have risked what I did for you," he reminded her, stung.

Suddenly she sounded weary, unlike Georgina. "I'm grateful for that, Tim, I really am. I won't ever forget it but"—and her voice grew cold again—"it was as much for your sake as mine, so don't let's get too sentimental."

The March morning was clear and cold and bright and the naked branches of a Kanzan cherry were black against a sky like stretched blue silk. The buds were fat on an ancient magnolia that leaned against the wall. A blackbird regarded them with head on one side, then flew away in sudden panic, low above the ground, chattering.

He began to speak again and she wondered with despair how she was going to be able to live with herself.

EIGHT

"That key will lead thee to a pretty secret."

THE GAIETY THEATRE was situated in Stockwell Lane, being part of a larger building, itself squashed into a narrow strip of land between the river and the road, with very little room either side. Officially this building was the Lavenstock Community Centre, because as well as housing the small theatre, it contained a large hall where dances and rock concerts, the occasional symphony concert and wedding receptions could be held, and smaller rooms where various local clubs such as the Camera Club and the local Writers' Circle held their meetings. Bingo was played there every Wednesday afternoon, and the premises were used for a toddlers' playgroup each Tuesday and Thursday morning. But its official name had never caught on; it would always be known locally as the Gaiety simply because the old theatre had been called that—the Gaiety, the one that had been pulled down to make way for the new shopping precinct, and still loudly mourned as a lost architectural gem by the Victorian Society who'd failed to save it. The inherited name of the present one bore no relation to its appearance, which was stark and modern and always reminded Mayo of nothing so much as an aircraft hangar.

Boards outside the box office informed the public that the next performance by the Thespians would be *The Changeling,* a Jacobean tragedy by Middleton and Rowley, a billing which caused Mayo to raise his eyebrows. They were only an amateur company, after all. But ambitious, seemingly.

"Oh, I don't know, they're supposed to have been going great guns since the Community Arts Director was appointed," Kite replied when he said as much.

"So that's why Doc Ison's been pressing me so hard to subscribe to a season ticket."

"He's been on at me too. Fat chance we'd have of getting here regularly! Anyway, it's not much in my line."

"This Cockayne's supposed to have been a professional actor, I gather?"

"Sort of. You know you've heard his name somewhere, you feel sure you've seen him on the telly, only you can't just remember in what . . ."

Kite went to try the door, while Mayo studied the prominently placed photograph of the Arts Director . . . Cockayne in typically flamboyant actorish stance, studied and self-aware, a comma of dark hair over his forehead, dark expressive eyes, his mouth slightly petulant. Handsome features, but basically unremarkable, the face of a thousand juvenile leads. Mayo wondered how long ago it had been taken, how much it resembled the present Ashleigh Cockayne. Well, he was about to find out.

"It's locked," Kite said. "Let's try the stage door."

That too proved to be locked, but there was still one more entrance at the back of the building they could try, where a terrace was cantilevered out over the river, with steps down to it and doors leading directly into the bar. Rounding the corner in order to try the other entrance, they came upon a builders' pick-up truck and a board propped against the wall announcing that Ron Prosser (Lavenstock) Ltd. was at work.

It seemed they had walked straight into an argument. Detectives both, they automatically came to a halt and listened to what was going on. The row appeared to be between Prosser—if he was the burly individual perched on a ladder and wearing a donkey jacket and woolly hat—and a small woman clad entirely in black. Her tiny, tapering figure, generous about the bust, slender on the hips, was wrapped in an outsize, hairy black poncho from which protruded two slender, elegant, black-stockinged legs finishing in high-heeled black suede shoes. "But it's too bad of you to disappear for a week, then choose to start again at the only time we have a daytime rehearsal!" she was declaring vehemently, perfectly colloquially, though with a slight accent which Mayo couldn't immediately place. "We can hardly hear ourselves speak . . . are you listening to what I'm telling you?"

Her hair, densely and improbably black, since the lady must have been sixty if she was a day, was scraped back like a ballerina's from a face which heavy make-up and a bright crimson slash of lipstick had made into a clown's. The man on the ladder regarded it imperturbably.

"Yo' want this job finishing, missis, yo'll have to put up with us," he returned, unmoved. "Think yersels lucky we'm working at all of a Saturday—which we shouldn't'a been only some clever dick's kept nicking me tackle. Fust one o' me ladders, next me gas bottle and a roll o' me roofing felt. Buggers round here'll tek anythink what isn't cemented down!"

"What's up, gaffer?" came a disembodied voice, followed by the face of a youth with a bleached, bristly head appearing over the parapet of the flat roof.

The man on the ladder and the woman ignored the interruption, the latter throwing out her hands widely and expressively at the incomprehensible chaos of builders' necessaries scattered around. Hosepipes. Wet cement. The ladders and a propane gas cylinder and a roll of roofing felt which presumably had been either retrieved or replaced.

"Perhaps if you didn't leave your things lying around to be tripped over they wouldn't *be* stolen," she declared, "and then you wouldn't have to work at the weekend, causing so much disturbance."

The builder put a foot on the ladder and gave her a long, considering look. "Sod off, missis," he said without rancour and began to climb, slowly and without haste. "Now, Justin, what yo' doing up there, besides minding other folks' business?"

The woman below looked savage and quite capable of replying in similar vein but then, her outrageously overdone costume earrings practically threatening to overbalance her, she spun round on her heel and began to march off. Mayo, who had never before seen this action performed outside the pages of fiction, watched fascinated. Halfway to the stage door she stopped abruptly, apparently only just becoming aware of the presence of the two watchers. "Yes? Was there something you were wanting?"

Annoyance put aside, she smiled at them, a melon-slice smile, and was transformed. Beautiful she was not at first or even second sight, but one might never be sure. What the French call *jolie-laide*, Mayo thought, and recognized that was what her accent was, French. "Can I help you?"

Mayo explained that they were looking for Mr. Ashleigh Cockayne, but it seemed they were due for a disappointment. "I'm afraid he's had to go to London rather urgently. Perhaps I can be of assistance. I'm standing in for him while he's away. My name is Lili Anand."

Mayo hesitated. He wasn't sure what this woman's position was and how much to tell her. She waited without speaking, watching him with bright, intelligent black eyes.

"We're police officers investigating the death of Mr. Rupert Fleming. I understand he was a friend of Mr. Cockayne's."

"Ah. Yes, I thought that was why you were here. Poor Rupert. Yes, he and Ashleigh were acquainted." The wind whipped round the corner, blowing the centrefold of last week's *Advertiser* into the river, flapping at the edges of the polythene under the builder's wet pile of cement. Lili Anand shivered suddenly and huddled herself deeper into her poncho. "Come inside where it's warmer. There's a rehearsal going on, but we shouldn't be long. We've nearly finished, and if you don't mind waiting, we can talk afterwards. I don't want to interrupt them. They've given up their Saturday afternoon after all, and they don't get paid for it."

Following her into the darkened auditorium, they slid into seats a few rows from the front. The stage was bare, the actors were in casual working clothes, mostly jeans and sweaters, and there was as yet no scenery in evidence. It wasn't easy to understand what they were up to on the stage, but after a while Mayo began to gather the threads. Powerful stuff, seemingly, a play full of dark obsessions, capable of degenerating into overdone melodrama if not handled properly, he suspected. A sombre and sinister story of intrigue and murder committed by an ill-favoured serving man at the instigation of his mistress against those who were an obstruction to what she desired. Kite shifted in his seat, nudged Mayo, whispered in his ear and nodded towards the stage.

Mayo nodded back to show he'd noticed too, and for a while continued to try to get to grips with the plot. But at last he aban-

doned it as a bad job and concentrated on the two principal actors.
The man who took the character of the ugly de Flores (an athletic,
handsome bloke who would presumably be suitably uglified for the
performance) was acting his socks off, his intention obviously being
not to be upstaged by the woman he was playing against. Didn't he
realize when he was beaten? He hadn't a hope, poor devil. She
would always outshine anyone else on stage because, apart from the
stunning impact of her physical presence, she knew what she was
about, she could really and truly *act*.

He should have known, Mayo told himself. She was born to it.
How far had she been playing a part when she'd told him she barely
knew Rupert Fleming? Was she yet another of his women? Along
with Georgina, Bryony, Lois?

He gave her his attention again, but nothing in her demeanour
gave him any clue. Whether she was aware of their presence in the
audience it was impossible to say, but if so, she certainly wasn't
letting it affect her performance. The beautiful Mrs. Susan Salisbury
had totally become Beatrice Joanna, a woman committed to evil,
whispering and entreating her besotted servant to perjure his soul
for her, and now refusing to pay the price of herself. Mayo, bedaz-
zled, followed her movements, light as thistledown, listened to her
voice, clear and innocent as an angel's: *"Thy language is so bold and
vicious, I cannot see which way I can forgive it with any modesty."*

And de Flores's answer: *"A woman dipped in blood, and talk of
modesty?"*

"She has the edge on them all, hasn't she, sir?" a voice next to him
whispered, and turning, Mayo saw that Janet Lindsay, whom he had
thought to be in Crete or Rhodes, had slipped into the seat beside
him. "She used to be a professional actress."

Unsurprised, Mayo reflected that the only wonder was that she
had abandoned what must have been a spectacular future for a man
like Tim Salisbury and the life of a farmer's wife, albeit a prosperous
one. No wonder she had turned to the Thespians, no doubt in an
endeavour to combat the dullness. And perhaps to Rupert Fleming?
She had given him to understand that their acquaintance had been
of the slightest, but she must have known him better than that,
surely, from his frequent visits to the Gaiety? He had put one of his

men onto finding out what he could about that putative relationship, but nothing had been turned up.

On stage, de Flores was declaiming: *". . . and made you one with me."*

"With thee, foul villain?"

"Yes, my fair murderess . . ."

"Try that once more," called Lili. "With slightly less sibilance, de Flores, if you please. We wouldn't want to go over the top, darling, now would we?"

Mayo turned to W.P.C. Lindsay and spoke to her in a low voice. "If you're not needed for a while, come outside, please. I'd like a word with you."

"I'm spare at the moment. I've been on the book, but they're word perfect by now so they don't need me," Janet whispered back, and he followed her as she slid from her seat.

Lili Anand saw them go from the corner of her eye but forced herself to keep her attention concentrated on the stage. When the scene came to an end she reluctantly wound up the rehearsal for that day. If she could have prolonged it, she would have done so. She'd known that, sooner or later, the police would be here and though she'd prepared what she was going to say to them, she was frightened at the thought of going through with it.

She'd begun to wish, these last few days, that she'd never come to Lavenstock, that the chance meeting with Ashleigh in Piccadilly had never happened. They hadn't seen each other for years, not since they'd worked together at the Winter Gardens in Malvern, and that had been more years ago than she was willing to admit. She'd always had a specially soft spot for Ashleigh. He enjoyed being mothered by her, and relished the boost her admiration gave to his fragile ego when he was feeling low, while he endeared himself to her by listening amiably to her stories of past triumphs and successes. Not that there'd been so many he hadn't heard them repeated over and over again. But he'd never so much as hinted that he found the repetition dull. All actors knew about the need for reassurance. He'd always been a good type, easy-going, if not particularly strong-minded.

He *had* been. Past tense. Lili wasn't so sure about either quality, now. People, like time and circumstances, change. The years hadn't brought Ashleigh the success he thought was due to him, the West End roles or the bland, television comedy parts he knew he would have excelled in, given the chance. He was thirty-seven, and he'd grown fed up of waiting. The recognition which he felt had always eluded him, the setbacks and disappointments, far from being character-forming as such things were supposed to be, seemed to have given him only a sense of grievance, a chip on the shoulder.

But when she'd met him in London and admitted that times were hard, and becoming harder, that she was due to lose the flat where she lived and that her agent hadn't had an offer of a part for her for over a year, he'd immediately turned up trumps and suggested she share the tiny house he had in Lavenstock. Actors were like that, generous when they were on the up, sticking together when they were down. As long as it suited them. She could help out with the productions at the Community Centre if she felt so inclined, he told her, and cook him those marvellous meals she was famous for. She'd jumped at the chance, though she was warned there could be no pay. But she had her pension now—a secret she kept well guarded— and as a Frenchwoman, though long-exiled, cooking came to her as easily as breathing. It was a small price to pay to be back in the world of theatre, even amateur theatre, and however peripherally.

Where *was* he?

She'd told the police he'd had to go to London suddenly and she was prepared to stick to her story for as long as she thought it might help him, which might not be for very much longer now, but that wasn't what had happened. The truth was he'd simply disappeared. She knew without being told that it was something to do with Rupert Fleming and an enormous fear clutched at her heart now as she sat where she was in the stalls, giving the police sergeant the names of the cast in case they might want to interview them, feeling every one of her sixty-four years.

She'd known that man Fleming was trouble the moment she met him. He'd blown into the theatre like an ill wind, or rather insinuated himself in, sneaking and ill-natured, like a chilling spiteful draught, cooling the warmth and good humour of the production, spoiling the enjoyment of those taking part. Trouble for Ashleigh

also, though when she'd mentioned this—cautiously, obliquely—
Ashleigh's furious silence had left her with the distinct impression
that she could mind her own business or pack her bags and go.
That's what she meant about his having changed. He'd never have
reacted like that in the old days. She'd grown more and more sure
the two men were involved in something underhand together. All
those late-night sessions at the theatre. And what about Trish? She
worried about that a lot.

And then, Ashleigh had simply vanished, without a word to her
or anyone else as far as she knew, and the next day Rupert had been
found dead. There was a sick, churned-up feeling in her stomach
whenever she thought about it, which was most of the time.

Janet Lindsay took Mayo with her into one of the small, empty
dressing rooms back-stage, where she switched on a small electric
fire. "I only got back from holiday yesterday, sir," she explained.
"And I didn't hear about Rupert Fleming until I got to the theatre. I
rang the station immediately to speak to you and they said you were
on your way here, so I waited for you. I'd like to help if I can."

"Aren't you still on leave?"

"That's all right, sir. I'm at a bit of a loose end, actually."

Mayo smiled. "If you put it that way, thank you—I understand
Fleming had connections here and it'll be useful if you can tell me
what you know about him, put me in the picture."

"I'll do my best, sir, but there isn't much. He wasn't a man who
gave out a lot about himself. The person who'd know most about
him is Ashleigh Cockayne. Fleming seemed to hang around here
quite a lot, sometimes during rehearsals, but mostly he came along
as they were ending. I couldn't make out why. It was nothing to do
with me, of course, nothing to do with anybody, he might simply
have been waiting to go out with Ashleigh for a drink or something
. . . and if it hadn't been for Trish I'd have tried to forget it."

"Who's Trish?"

"Diaphanta, the waiting woman in the play who also gets murdered. The red-haired girl, Trish Lambert. Did you notice her, sir?"

He'd have been blind if he hadn't. A young girl, seventeen or
eighteen at a guess, bursting out of her skin-tight jeans like a ripe fig,

giving out provocative sexual signals from under her eyelashes. A taut bottom that ought to be thoroughly spanked. A long fall of shining red-gold hair.

"Red at the moment," Janet amended thoughtfully. "She keeps changing the colour and the style."

"Why were you worried about her? Was Fleming pestering her?" Though the girl was unlikely to have let that bother her overmuch, he'd have bet, from the little he'd seen of her.

"No, at least I don't think so, but you could never tell with Fleming . . . he always had some woman or other in tow, different women, you know. I had the impression he used to string them along and then drop them suddenly when he got fed up. But I don't know about Trish. She's still at school, but she wants to act professionally. She's not bad, really, for her age, I suppose. She'll never be anywhere near as good as Susan, mind, but if determination will get her anywhere, she'll succeed. Although in some ways, she's rather a silly girl."

Having delivered herself of this Janet, rather prosaic young woman that she was, sat back, suddenly feeling distressingly like her own strait-laced Scottish grannie. Had she let her imagination run away with her? Or her Presbyterian conscience? After all, as she'd remarked to Mitch, what had there been to go on? Trish staying on after the others had left, waiting for a lift home, or so she said, from Ashleigh. Refusing Janet's own offer to drive her home. A feeling that she was up to the neck in something with the pair of them, though Janet had always felt that Fleming, in fact, seemed to find the girl mildly tiresome. It was difficult to explain, but now that she'd spoken, she'd have to have a go.

"I tried to have a word with her, but she wouldn't listen. She just shrugged and walked away. And there really wasn't anything definite."

"Leave her to me, I'll have a talk with her. But come on, Janet, what did you *think* was going on?"

Janet tried to remember that she was a policewoman first, a Presbyterian second, and told him.

NINE

"I have kiss'd poison for't, strok'd a serpent."

LILI FELT she'd hung around long enough while the Chief Inspector interviewed that feather-brained Trish. Her high heels were killing her and she badly wanted to kick them off, put her feet up and lie back with a cup of tea at her elbow. So she simply picked up the big canvas holdall from which she was inseparable and told one of the cast she was off and if the police had a mind to talk to her, they'd find her at home.

Home was a small house in a short street of nineteenth-century workmen's cottages that sloped down to the river, not far from the Gaiety. A very long time had passed since The Leasowes had been the pasture from which the street derived its name. Now, smart white paint, window boxes and ruffled blinds were evidence of proud home ownership, the Renaults and Sierras parked outside in the street gave status to the occupants. The house which Ashleigh Cockayne rented at the top of the street was a little different. It had been recently repainted by the Council when it was offered as an inducement to secure a Community Arts Director for the town, but they hadn't run to window boxes and Ashleigh's taste wasn't for Austrian blinds.

It was a tiny house: one room, a kitchen and a scullery downstairs, two bedrooms and a bathroom above, but big enough to accommodate Lili as an extra as well as Ashleigh, since the way their lives had been lived had taught them not to demand too much space, and not so large that a fairly total disinterest in any form of housekeeping would result in chaos. It had been minimally furnished by the Council and embellished by the personal clutter with which each defined themselves. It was a home. Lili thankfully eased off her shoes, boiled the kettle, switched on the gas fire and settled herself in like a snail into its shell.

Mayo meanwhile was talking to Trish Lambert, leaving Kite to chat to the rest of the cast over coffee, which came black, bitter and boiling in Styrofoam beakers, full of promise to keep them all on their toes. Hopefully, Kite would get them talking. It was to his advantage that he looked ingenuous and younger than his years, with a ready smile and open manner, which he knew how to exploit. Few people realized his acuity until it was too late.

Janet Lindsay had with some difficulty at last managed to produce Trish. When she knew the police wanted to speak to her the girl had locked herself in one of the lavatories and for fifteen minutes had refused to come out. Eventually persuaded by Janet's calm reasonableness that she couldn't stay there all day, she emerged, enveloped in a big, loose sweater that covered her nearly to the knees and merely hinted at the sexy curves beneath. She'd been crying and her make-up had worn off, revealing a crop of freckles on the bridge of her nose and her cheekbones. She was very pale and looked about eleven years old, with the sullen look of a guilty child, and when she heard she was going to be questioned by the Chief Inspector himself, she became, it seemed to him, frightened, too. But there was nothing of this in her first words: "I haven't done anything wrong. Why d'you want to ask *me* questions, and none of the others?"

"We may yet want to question them all. There's nothing to be afraid of, just tell the truth, that's all. You know that Rupert Fleming is dead, and what we need to do is trace his movements. It seems likely you were one of the last people to see him alive."

"Me?"

"You had a rehearsal on Monday evening?"

"That's no secret."

"And afterwards you stayed on while the rest of the cast left."

"So? There's no law against it." She had decided cheekiness was to be her best defence, but that didn't worry Mayo. It wasn't any more than he'd expected. Nine out of ten kids he had to question reacted in the same way, especially when they'd something to hide.

"Why did you stay, Trish? What was the reason?"

"Can't we stop talking about me? What I did or didn't do's my business."

"Ours too now, I'm afraid. What happened when you stayed behind? Please explain as clearly as you can."

"Explanations are so *boring.*"

"I expect I can stand it."

"If you must know," she said after a truculent pause, "Ashleigh asked me to stay behind to have supper with him. He was going to take me to the Rose." She gave the name of Lavenstock's only night-club, throwing out the information with a studied casualness that didn't come off, as though it was quite natural that she of all the cast had been accorded the favour, picked out from the other women members by an older, sophisticated man. Well, she didn't have to be intelligent, as well as sexy. And she was still very young.

Just how young, Mayo was genuinely surprised to find, when he asked her. "Fifteen," she answered sulkily.

He waited, eyeing her gravely before saying deliberately, "Did your mother know what you were doing, staying out till all hours?"

The colour flared into her face, then receded. "I haven't a mother. They're divorced. But listen"—and now panic lifted her voice—"you're not to tell my father . . . he'd kill me!"

"How is it he doesn't know what time you get home?"

"He's at work. He works nights. He's a security man at Leverson's."

Poor devil, thought Mayo, empathizing with the absent father, knowing from firsthand experience the pitfalls and terrors of bringing up a teenage daughter alone. But of all the jobs Lambert could have chosen, that surely was the worst. Didn't he realize the extent of the problem he had in this daughter of his? Mayo experienced a momentary, unexpected plummet of the heart. Supposing if, after all, he thought, imagining Julie, who had grown more subtle, less understandable as she grew older . . . then he smiled to himself, knowing his Julie, or thinking he did, and brought his mind back.

"You're alone in the house all night?" he asked.

"I'm not a child!"

"Old enough to know what you were doing?" She tossed her head, looking away, and he sighed. "Would you find it easier to talk to Miss Lindsay on your own?"

"I don't care, it's all the same to me."

Mayo made a sign to Janet, who took a deep breath and asked gently, "All right, it was photographs, wasn't it, Trish? Photographs that Cockayne took, and then developed here in the Camera Club's darkroom?"

The quick colour again came into her face, turning it a sullen red. "If you know so much, why're you asking me?"

"But I'm right, aren't I?" The girl lapsed into a stubborn silence. "Aren't I, Trish?"

"If I tell you, you won't tell my dad, will you?" she mumbled at last.

"That depends whether you tell us the truth or not." The response was another mulish silence.

"He *was* taking pictures of you, wasn't he, Trish? The sort you wouldn't want to show to your family and friends?" Janet prompted.

"What if he was?" she burst out. "They weren't—well, you know what I mean, nothing kinky. Ashleigh's not like that, they were for art and photography magazines . . . he said they'd help my career, he's promised he'll use them to try and get me into films." Sweeping her red hair over her shoulder, she said, her chin lifting, "If you've a good body, why be ashamed of showing it?"

Mayo looked at this child, younger than his own daughter in more than years. He felt very tired. "Let's hear all about it, Trish."

But the extent of her knowledge was limited to her posing for the pictures here at the theatre, after the rest of the cast had gone and the other organisations had finished for the night. Cockayne had used his own camera and availed himself of the facilities of the Camera Club's darkroom to develop the pictures. Sometimes they used some of the props. After that, it had been up to Rupert Fleming.

Mayo caught Janet's eye and she nodded imperceptibly. Trish's words confirmed everything that had made her suspicious: certain props for which she'd been responsible having been disturbed, the camera which Cockayne was so touchy about when she'd expressed interest, those late nights . . . it had all seemed too add up.

"Did he ever bring any other girls to be photographed, Trish?" Mayo asked.

"No way!"

She was indignant, naive enough to believe herself unique, but there'd have been others. Who, when and where would emerge, he thought grimly, remembering those rather more than nasty girlie mags they'd found in Fleming's drawer. He'd nothing but contempt for a sordid little operation of this sort, using under-age girls, selling their bodies to promote dirt like that in low-grade skin magazines for what must have been precious little reward. The more he discovered about Rupert Fleming, the less pity he felt for his untimely and horrible end.

"All right, Trish. Let's talk about what happened on Monday, after the rehearsal. You stayed behind and Mr. Cockayne began taking pictures of you, right?"

"No, I've told you, we were going out for supper that night. Besides—" She checked herself and slid him a glance before hurrying on, evidently thinking better of what she'd been going to say. "I waited for Ashleigh in his office while he checked that everyone had left and got the keys from Ernest Underwood."

"Ernest Underwood? Who's he?"

"The caretaker. He can't go home at night until he's handed the keys over to Ashleigh."

"I see. Go on."

"Ashleigh'd just got back with the keys when Rupert Fleming came in. He'd been watching the rehearsal but we both thought he'd gone home. Ashleigh was really mad and asked him why he was hanging around. He told him we were going out and if Rupert wanted to see him he'd just have to come back the next day."

"Didn't that surprise you—that he should speak to Mr. Fleming like that? After all, they were supposed to be good friends, weren't they?" She shrugged. "What was Fleming's reaction?"

"He said, 'Come on, let's have a drink and forget about all that, Ashleigh. It's water under the bridge.' Ashleigh said, 'That's not the way I see it,' and they started arguing. I couldn't make out what they were on about, it was really boring, and then Ashleigh suddenly gave in. He said all right, if that was what Rupert wanted. And that was it."

"D'you mean Fleming left after that?"

"No!" The girl flushed with remembered chagrin. "It was *me* who had to leave! I was choked off by then and I asked them what about me, and Rupert said there's always a taxi, ask Ashleigh to get you one. So he did, he took me down and got me one from the rank round the corner. I could see he was really sorry about everything, having to cancel our supper and that, and he promised we'd go another time, but I was furious. Well, it wasn't very nice, was it? All because of Rupert Fleming barging in!"

"I can see why you were upset. Didn't Cockayne explain what it was all about?"

"Only that it wasn't his fault, but they'd things to talk about that couldn't be put off. He laughed in ever such a funny way, but he told me not to worry, he'd make sure Rupert Fleming didn't spoil any more of our little outings."

Mayo caught Janet's glance. "Have you any idea at all—can you make guess, even—what it was all about, this quarrel between the two of them?"

She looked away. "No."

"Sure, Trish?"

"Well, I guess—I suppose it *may* have been something to do with . . . well, Ashleigh'd decided he wasn't going to take any more pictures. Not just yet anyway . . . I don't suppose Rupert would've been very pleased about that, exactly."

Mayo studied her, unable to make up his mind whether she was quite as naive as she sounded. "Was it a sudden decision, to give up taking them?"

"Not really. That was why he was taking me out," she said in a sudden burst of candour, "to make up for there being no more sessions."

"He gave no reasons?"

"He said we mustn't flood the market. We used to try to make me look different, different hairstyles and that but—he just thought we ought to give it a rest for a bit."

Mayo considered her, until her eyes dropped under his unflinching stare. He was a case-hardened copper and he couldn't believe that Cockayne had restricted himself simply to taking pictures of the girl. He'd a hell of a lot to be responsible for, this Cockayne, no wonder he'd scarpered.

"I'd like to go back to Monday, Trish. What was your impression of Mr. Fleming when he came up to Cockayne's office? How did he seem?"

"Oh, no worse than usual. I mean, he was always a pain. Oh, all right, I know that's not a very nice thing to say about somebody who's dead, and I suppose he was okay, if you like that sort—but he always acted so superior. He looked at a person as though they were dirt. Not a bit like Ashleigh. He's really, really nice." Her face suddenly flushed, she looked down at her hands, the hands of a little girl, small and ringless, the nails badly bitten. "I'm sorry I was mad at him, now. When's he coming back?" she asked in a small voice.

Mayo said, making his voice kind, "Probably soon, Trish. And thank you, you've really been a very good witness."

"Can I go now?" He said she could and she sprang up with relief. At the door, she paused. "You won't tell my dad, will you?"

"I promise he won't hear a thing from us unless it's absolutely necessary."

That didn't make her a lot happier, but it wasn't intended to. He hadn't finished with Trish yet. She'd had a fright, and it might pull her up short for a while, but girls like her needed a bit more than that. If they wanted to go to the devil, they would, and there wasn't a lot you could do about it, but she hadn't yet gone so far along the road that there was no chance of turning her around to face the way she'd come.

"What are you afraid of, Miss Anand?"

"Oh, Lili, *please!* No one ever calls me anything else."

Mayo had been talking to her for fifteen minutes before he eventually found the opportunity to ask the question that had been hovering on his lips ever since he began. By many circuitous routes they'd reached the point where she had admitted that Cockayne, far from being in London on business, had disappeared to all intents and purposes into thin air. She was now leaning back in her chair with her tiny feet on a footstool in an attitude of exaggerated exhaustion, her eyes half-closed, her hand to her forehead. On her forefinger was a heavy silver ring with a black stone of some sort, the size of a knuckle-duster. The histrionics would have amused Mayo, had the circumstances been different, but not now, he reflected, repeating the question and waiting for his answer.

"Afraid?" Her response was a little too alert for the pose she'd adopted. Under the shade of her hand, the glance of her bright black eyes had sharpened their focus.

"Huh-huh."

He allowed the silence to grow until she suddenly swooped her hand down and pulled from the big canvas bag at her side a large piece of colourful tapestry stretched on a wooden frame, into which she began stabbing a needle threaded with bright wool. Emerging on the canvas was what appeared to be a woodland scene, with small animals and birds, squirrels, a pheasant, rabbits, a snail and a butterfly jostling in unlikely juxtaposition among jewel-coloured flowers of equally improbable association. The needle flew in and out several times, then her hand stopped its stitching and dropped to her lap. Their eyes met and she said in a trembling voice that forgot all its years of speech training, "Oh dear God, I'm so afraid he might have killed himself."

"Cockayne? Killed himself? Why should you imagine that?"

"Imagine? You call it imagination if you want . . . I wouldn't." She drew a deep breath before continuing more calmly, "He once said to me—we were watching the TV news and some murderer had been given a life sentence—and he said, 'If ever they wanted to put me away for life I'd drown myself, before being shut away like that, I swear I would.' "

"He used those specific words?"

"The very same," she averred solemnly, and he didn't doubt they were. Her memory would be excellent, trained to remember every word and nuance. "He said it had to be the best way. Just jump in the water and let go."

Mayo raised his eyebrows. Easy to talk. Not so easy to find the courage when it came to it.

"Oh, you can look like that, but he meant it, you can be sure of that. And besides—" She paused to give him a sideways, assessing glance, then decided to go on. "Besides, I saw it in the Tarot."

"The Tarot. Ah."

He'd no patience with superstition and the dangerous games

played with it, and she saw that. Her black eyes gleamed to equal those of the squirrel she had fashioned. "Don't despise the Tarot, Mr. Mayo. I've seen more things there than you'd believe. Last week, I saw La Mort."

The sign of Death, wasn't that?

He knew they were a superstitious lot, theatre folk, but this was going a bit far. Maybe she believed it or maybe she knew more than she was saying. "Let's get this clear. What you're really saying, Lili . . . you think Ashleigh Cockayne murdered Rupert Fleming?"

"Am I? Well, then, perhaps I am." Her voice trembled but her hands began again, darting among the fantasy on her canvas. "But if he did, it was no more than Fleming deserved because I am telling you," she said, suddenly very French, "there were times when I could have killed him myself. And I'll tell you something else . . . I am glad he is dead." She smiled and drove her needle through the eye of a robin.

He followed the progress of her sewing in silence for a while. "I think," he said, "there's something you're not telling me."

Her eyes met his consideringly, then she sighed. "I knew I should have to tell you some time. They'd had a row, and Ashleigh . . . well, one thing you must know—it wasn't temper. He'd never let fly, but I'm afraid he could sulk. He could bear a grudge, let things smoulder for weeks until the time when he could get his own back."

"What was it all about, this row they had?"

"I don't know. He came home in such a state one evening last week—"

"Which evening?"

"I don't remember which—oh yes, Wednesday, it must have been Wednesday."

So that was when the row had begun, and it had lasted until the following Monday, the same evening that Trish had had her date with Ashleigh Cockayne so rudely cancelled, when Fleming had arrived at the theatre to make up the quarrel with Cockayne.

"He was still a bag of nerves," Lili went on, "right through the weekend. In the end I asked him what was the matter and he said, 'Oh God, Lili, I wish I could tell you, but I can't. This is a decision I've got to make for myself. I'm in it up to the neck and it's either me or that bastard Fleming.' That was Monday evening, when he said that, before the rehearsal, and when I got up the next morning he'd gone—no note, nothing."

"Fleming was there at the Monday rehearsal, I believe?"

"Yes, he came in when we'd nearly finished, as he usually did. Sat in the front and waited, watching the women, as always. I could see Ashleigh didn't like it, but it wasn't any business of mine. They were two grown men, they had to sort it out between them, whatever was bothering them."

"Did you think it was about a woman, this row they'd had? Fleming seems to have known a few. Susan Salisbury, maybe?"

"Susan?" She laughed shortly and rethreaded her needle. The robin was finished. A bluebell had begun to blossom under her hand. "You're like all men, you think just because a woman looks like Susan, she's available. Take it from me, she's not."

He said mildly, "Not me, I don't think that, but maybe Fleming did."

"No, no. You're on the wrong lines there."

"All the same, Mrs. Salisbury interests me. What sort of future did she have, as a professional actress?"

"Who can tell? She's very gifted, and with those looks she'd have got to the top one way or another, bound to, and maybe in time she'd have become a great actress as well. But it's a hard life and you need more than a bit of talent and a pretty face. Here of course she's a star, but how she'd have shaped up professionally . . ." Her shoulders lifted in a Gallic shrug and she gave him an assessing glance. "How old do you think she is?"

He replied without thinking too much about it, "Twenty-six, twenty-seven?"

It was what came to mind and yet he wasn't altogether too surprised when she said, "She's nearly forty. You've been to her home, she tells me. Have you seen her husband?"

"Yes, I've met him."

"Well, then." He raised his eyebrows and she spelled out, "Susan likes it easy, Mr. Mayo, and Tim Salisbury's very comfortably off. She laps up admiration and he gives it. But more than anything, she adores those two lovely children of hers. She wanted babies more than she wanted fame. Before it was too late."

As he reflected on that, another thought recurred to him. Despite their apparent difference in age, Salisbury was evidently besotted by his wife. Supposing he'd discovered, or imagined he'd discovered, some sort of liaison between her and Fleming? Supposing all this stuff about Cockayne's quarrel with Fleming was smokescreening the real truth? Fiveoaks Farm was near enough to where Fleming had been found, near enough to have been a lovers' trysting place. Supposing Tim Salisbury had come across them, and shot Fleming?

There should have been a check made on Tim Salisbury's movements that night, he'd given orders to have that done, and presumably it had tallied with what he said he'd been doing, but he'd have another look at it when he got back to Milford Road. But he wasn't pinning much faith on the idea. For one thing, there was the gun, Culver's gun. They always came back to that. And the whisky and the barbiturates.

He went back to Lili and his original line of questioning. "They'd always been good friends up until this row they had, Cockayne and Fleming?"

"Oh no, never *friends,* I think. Acquaintances would be a better word, perhaps business partners in some way, but how should I know? Ashleigh didn't discuss their relationship with me, I wouldn't have expected it."

He thought this might not be quite true. In the normal way he guessed there would certainly have been at least one or two agreeably gossipy sessions during which Fleming's character and propensities would have been taken apart and scrutinised. Wasn't that the way with theatre people, with most people come to that, given the chance—and it was probably his failure to do so which had excited her curiosity as much as anything else. "Fleming never came to the house," she continued. "Whatever it was they had to do with each other it was conducted there, at the Gaiety."

"Do you have any idea what that was?"

She shook her head but looked away, not meeting his eyes. She wasn't ready to talk about that; she'd said enough, her attitude conveyed, more than enough. They'd find out, but not from her.

She didn't know it, but her secrecy was wasted now. Mayo didn't feel it expedient to say so. He wanted evidence of those pictures, if any still existed, and he told Lili there would have to be a search made of the house.

"Go ahead. You won't find anything," she said, meeting his glance without fear or favour. So either she had searched, herself, and found nothing, or had got rid of anything incriminating. Not deliberately obstructive, Lili, but too well-intentioned towards Ashleigh Cockayne to be of further help at the moment, he thought.

"One more thing," he said as he rose to go. "Did Cockayne ever take sleeping pills?"

"Sleeping pills?" Her eyes widened in surprise and then she laughed in rather an odd way, saying no, he didn't ever need *sleeping pills,* as far as she knew.

"Do you?"

"Once in a blue moon."

At his request she went to look for what she had and brought back a half-full bottle. She took them so infrequently, she said, that she'd no idea how many, if any at all, were missing. Mayo took the bottle with him and she asked him no questions about why he should want it.

"You should remember what I said about Rupert Fleming," she told him before he went, "I didn't like him and he didn't like me. I was too old for one thing, too old for him to be able to get round me with sex, like he did with the others. But he was a mischief-maker. He liked to set people against one another. You ask anyone. Ask de Flores—ask Greg Foster."

TEN

"Oh, but instinct is of a subtler strain."

A BRIGHT, BLOWY MORNING it turned out to be on Sunday, the best sort of March day. The mad wind bowling last night's take-away cartons as merrily as tumbleweed along the gutters, the bells of St. Nicholas's Parish church summoning those still of the faithful. Most of the investigating team, including Mayo, could think of more than one thing they'd rather be doing than sitting here in a small stuffy office separated from the busy incident room by a glass partition, drinking canteen coffee, comparing notes and reports and waiting for their briefing. Washing their cars, for instance, putting up shelves, playing golf, taking the wife and kids for an outing. All wishful thinking at this stage in the proceedings. The hunt for Ashleigh Cockayne was under way.

During his time in Lavenstock, he appeared to have made no friends other than those connected with the Thespians. He had no living relatives, Lili said. On the other hand, there were theatre friends all over the country who would have taken him in with casual generosity, accepting only the vaguest of reasons for his wanting a temporary lodging. Crises in their own chancy lives happened all the time—and who cared for listening to boring and lengthy explanations as to how they'd come about?

Where had he last worked? Mayo wanted to know.

Somewhere in the north, Lili thought, but she couldn't be sure. She knew someone who might, though . . . she gave them names, addresses, phone numbers.

Meanwhile, a search had been made of his office at the Community Centre and the house at The Leasowes, revealing nothing more incriminating than a dubious taste in fancy underwear and a tendency to sloppiness and carelessness over his personal belongings. Well, Mayo hadn't expected that he would be so foolish as to leave proof of his suspect photographic activities, for instance, lying around to be picked up, either at home or at the theatre. However careless he'd been about other things, he'd always been meticulous when using the darkroom of the Camera Club in the basement for his developing, and the members had never had any cause to suspect any illicit use of their equipment. But he'd sailed on the windy side of the law regarding that activity, Mayo thought savagely, and he'd have him for it, be it the last thing he did—though that would be the least of Cockayne's worries if he were found now. He'd covered his tracks well, if that had been his intention. If Cockayne was their man. The odds were increasing that he was.

Mayo perched on the edge of a table, facing the view of the grimy, graceless Town Hall, a view dismally familiar and marginally worse from here on the ground floor than it was from his office window on the floor above. One thing about the Town Hall, though, it was an encouragement to the mind to think of other things. He hitched himself further onto the table and, for the benefit of the whole team, began summing up as far as they'd got, ticking the facts off on his fingers as he did so.

The two men, Fleming and Cockayne, had been in cahoots over the dirty picture business. At some time during the previous week they'd had a row, cause unspecified, which still hadn't been resolved by the following Monday evening, when Fleming had again come to the Gaiety after the rehearsal, but this time with the intention of apologizing and making his peace with Cockayne. His overtures hadn't at first been well received. What had followed could only be conjecture, apart from two indisputable facts: one, Fleming had been murdered, two, Cockayne had disappeared. Ergo, find Cockayne, find the murderer. Q.E.D.

On the face of it, simple. So why did he still have this persistent nag that it was *not* as simple as that? That something was wrong with this whole business?

"What about the gun, sir?" asked D.C. Farrar, looking bright and alert as a squirrel on the lookout for nuts.

"It bothers me, lad, that, it bothers me a lot."

"Dodgy, whichever way you look at it," Kite agreed. "If Cockayne's our man, why *John Culver's* gun?"

"Maybe because he was the only person Cockayne knew who owned one. Perhaps Fleming had mentioned at some time that his father-in-law owned several. So Cockayne went along and pinched it," Farrar suggested.

"Wouldn't have been difficult," Kite allowed. "If Culver's to be believed, it didn't go missing until after eleven on Sunday morning when he finished cleaning his guns. We've checked with the house-keeper and she went home at about half past four on Monday—leaving the door unlocked because Culver was still out and is too damned stubborn to admit he's got anything worth pinching. If Cockayne'd been keeping watch from the woods behind the house for an opportunity, that would've been it."

"No problem getting into the *house,* but what about the windows to the gun room? Too small to get in by, and the door showed no signs of being forced," Mayo reminded him. "So either Cockayne didn't pinch the gun, or he got hold of it some other way. Don't forget either that he didn't *know* Fleming was going to appear at the Gaiety on Monday night. He'd made arrangements to take young Trish out to supper."

"If he already had the gun and the intention, he might have just taken the opportunity, sir," Farrar said, which was sharp of him, thought Mayo, remembering Lili's contention that Cockayne could brood and bide his time.

"Or maybe," Spalding offered, encouraged by the approving nod Mayo had given the other young D.C., *"Fleming* pinched it to shoot Cockayne with and Cockayne got it off him somehow and used it against him."

"And maybe Culver *gave* the gun to Cockayne to get rid of Fleming," Atkins put in dryly. "Come on, lads, we can do better than that!"

There were plenty of ifs and buts, Mayo agreed, and skirmishing around them like this was apt to make him impatient. It did no harm to bat theories around, though. That way they might hit on a possibility no one had thought of before. At the moment, however, nobody was scoring bull's-eyes.

"Never mind the details at this stage," he said. "Let's concentrate on the broad outline." He leafed through the sheaf of notes in his hand. It appeared that although Cockayne had apparently taken nothing else at all with him, he *had* taken his car from the bit of vacant ground behind The Leasowes where he kept it.

"He could be halfway to outer space by now," someone muttered gloomily.

"Not if he's gone in *that* car," Kite said. "It's a beat-up old S Reg VW Beetle and he hasn't driven it for months until now. Didn't pass its last M.O.T. and was hardly worth the cost of repairing. We'll soon have it picked up."

"Who checked that coppice just off the road?" Mayo asked. "Where that footpath from Scotley Beeches leads to? Wasn't it you, Farrar?"

"Yes, sir," Farrar said. "Me and Deeley. You could park a car there, no problem, there's a little clearing behind some bushes. But there was no hope of finding any traces. Some sort of heavy machinery, probably a farm tractor or something like that, had recently turned round in the gateway and it was like a ploughed field. It's in my report, sir," he added with as much reproof in his tone as he dared, reminding Mayo of the pile of other reports on his desk, waiting to be read.

"Pity."

If this had been a murder deliberated on by Cockayne, not a spur-of-the-moment killing, he must surely have made provision for getting away, left his car stashed away somewhere ready to pick up, and that had been the obvious place. There could be others, but few as convenient. Otherwise he would have been obliged to walk home via the main road, back to pick up his car. Maybe seven or eight miles, a couple of miles less as the crow flew. But Cockayne didn't have wings and in direct line there would have been farmers' fields and woods, muddy streams, a stretch of electrified railway line and then suburban gardens to negotiate. No, if he'd walked, unlikely as it seemed, it would have been via the road.

"Keep looking out for any other place he might've parked, lads. And put out a call for anyone who saw a man walking on the Lavenstock Road that night, George," he said to Atkins. "Somebody must have seen him if he walked, maybe even given him a lift. It's only a minor road but a lot of drivers use it as a short cut to the main Stratford Road."

He broke the meeting up shortly after that, removing himself from the scene and going upstairs, through the busy, orderly incident room with the jangling telephones and the flashing screens of the word processors, the clacking typewriters and the constant comings and goings of shirt-sleeved officers. There was work a-plenty to be done while Cockayne was located.

The Stockwell was a longish river, if you added its length to the Avon, which it joined after about thirty miles, but if Cockayne's body was in it, it should turn up, sooner or later. Why, though, the Stockwell? Any old river would have done just as well to drown in. Or any canal, pond, lake or reservoir, anywhere in the country, come to that. *If* he had drowned himself. He didn't have to have done away with himself that way. He didn't have to be dead.

And yet . . .

Lili was sure that Cockayne was no longer alive. She had a shrewd intelligence, plus intuition, and never mind the Tarot cards, he wasn't inclined to dismiss the idea out of hand. Police work was ninety-nine percent hard slog, leg-work, method and routine, but intuition played its part occasionally and you ignored it at your peril. His sceptical policeman's mind rejected the idea as a total solution, however. And life, he'd found, when it came to the crunch, was precious, even to a murderer, even to an Ashleigh Cockayne. "If ever that would happen to me," Cockayne had said to Lili, perhaps subconsciously admitting that enough violence was contained within himself to enable such a possibility to exist. If ever that should happen, he'd sworn to kill himself . . . though not apparently through remorse, or from sorrow that he should have taken another human life, but simply because he couldn't bear the thought of his own personal freedom being curtailed through long, mournful years. That he might have had second thoughts, when it came to the moment of truth, Mayo thought entirely possible.

But if Lili *was* right, and he *had* committed suicide, his reasons for killing Fleming might never be revealed, and Fleming's demise might well go down as one of the unsolved murders of our time. It could happen, but it wasn't a possibility Mayo was going to admit until he had to. Meanwhile, the big question was: where was he—or his body?

Kite was bogged down, still making telephone calls, when Mayo stopped for lunch, so he took himself down to the Saracen's Head for a solitary ploughman's, using the time for some constructive thought. When he'd finished, he made a circuitous route back to Milford Road, by way of the Gaiety.

"Community Arts Director?" Ernest Underwood said, stacking black plastic bags full of Saturday night's rubbish outside the building's back door. "Wouldn't pay him in washers, I wouldn't!"

What exactly his qualifications were for making such a sweeping statement wasn't clear. He was a short, muscular man of about sixty-five, with a bald head, a small moustache and a disagreeable air of self-importance. He wore a short brown holland smock over a pair of black dress trousers, a Viyella check shirt and a Lavenstock College tie to which he was almost certainly not entitled.

Mayo said, "I believe it's Mr. Cockayne's practice to collect the keys from you at night before you go home, and to see to the final locking up himself?"

"Sometimes he does, sometimes he don't."

"What's that supposed to mean?"

"Depends on whether he remembers or not. Careless he is. All the same, these actor types. Airy fairy."

"You mean that sometimes doors are left unlocked all night?"

"No, I don't!" Underwood replied, scandalised. "Locked every night, they are, because I lock 'em meself. It's my responsibility. I said to him only last week, 'Look 'ere,' I said, 'who's responsible for this place at night, you or me? If it's you, fair enough. But if it's me, I want everybody out before I lock up and go home, and that includes you.' He knew what I meant." He spun one of the bags expertly round and tightly secured the resultant twist with a knot. "Excuse me, got to get these outside."

The Council wouldn't be coming to collect rubbish on a Sunday afternoon, for sure, but Ernest Underwood didn't appear to be the man to leave undone today what he could easily do tomorrow.

"Come on, Mr. Underwood, you can't expect *me* to know what he meant," Mayo said patiently. "Be a bit clearer, won't you?"

"He wouldn't have that, oh no, wouldn't want me hanging around waiting until he decides to go home. Does he think I don't know what's going on when he's here till all hours, and not by hisself, neither? Does he think I go round with me eyes closed? Does he think I was born yesterday?" Evidently none of these questions required an answer. " 'You just lock up every night and give me the keys and your responsibility's over,' he says, but it don't work like that. All that fuss last week about that builder's stuff what went missing . . . well, it was *me* your lot questioned about it, not him, and I take a dim view of that. I take a very dim view."

Sunday or not, there were plenty of activities going on at the Community Centre. A game of Ping-Pong was in process in one of the rooms; from somewhere in the distance the peculiarly tuneless singing of very young children could be heard, accompanied by a piano, some sort of Sunday school class, perhaps.

"So I decided after that," Underwood went on self-importantly, as the children reached an uncoordinated end, "that however long Mr. Cocky Cockayne decided to stay of a night, I'd still be here. I'd give him the keys and tell him I was off home, but I wouldn't go, not me. Not until after he did, any road, and I'd checked everything was safe. I have me little cubby-hole to stay in and I have me pass keys, so that's what I did."

Ernest Underwood was that type of person who takes pleasure in thwarting anybody who stands in higher authority than he does himself. Ashleigh Cockayne would have done better to have kept on the right side of him. A dangerous little man, thought Mayo, not by any means convinced by the reasons Underwood had given for staying on. Men like him didn't put in voluntary unpaid overtime, not unless they had cogent reasons for doing so—like doing a little bit more snooping on his own account, for instance.

"What was going on then, after the rehearsals?"

"Hanky-panky," Underwood declared, but by the way he blustered when pressed to be more explicit, Mayo knew the caretaker had no real idea.

"All right, if you'd decided to stay behind, you must still have been here on Monday night when Mr. Cockayne left?"

Underwood nodded. "And Fleming. Waited till I saw 'em drive off together in that there red Porsche. Put the light off in me cubbyhole and watched them. Ten past eleven it was. I remember thinking good job I'd brought me bike, 'cos I'd missed the last bus while they was upstairs knocking it back, though they wasn't as late as usual."

"Been drinking, had they? Sure about that?"

Underwood gave him a pitying smile. "Very fond of a drop, our Mr. Ashleigh, always keeps a bottle of Scotch in his cupboard." So Cockayne was a heavy drinker, was he? This would explain, perhaps, what Lili had meant about not needing sleeping pills. "Besides," Underwood went on, "they was none too steady on their feet, neither of 'em, when they crossed the car park, I can tell you. Couldn't hardly stand up."

"And you didn't feel you ought to try and stop them driving?"

"Not up to me," said Underwood.

Fleming, of course, was unused to drink in any quantity, never mind laced with barbiturates, so because he was probably already incapable, Cockayne would have been staggering too as he supported him to the car, before taking the wheel and driving him out to Scotley Beeches. This still left open a large query as to why Cockayne should just happened to have had those sleeping pills handy—not to mention a shotgun. Moreover, there hadn't been any whisky in Cockayne's office when it was searched, and Mayo told Underwood so.

"Because I'd thrown the empty bottle away, hadn't I?" Underwood retorted, a malicious light of triumph in his eyes. "No use keeping empty bottles. It's my job to see everything's cleaned up and left nice and tidy. I do the office meself, can't trust these women. Lick and a promise, that's all they're up to. I threw it in his waste basket before it was emptied, washed the glasses up and took them back."

Mayo gave up for the time being. He wasn't going to get anything more out of Underwood. He knew what he'd seen, and what he thought about it, and you'd never get him to go back on that, even if he were proved wrong. You couldn't tell a man like this anything. He'd continue to believe that the bomb would never drop, and know that everyone else was wrong, while the crack of doom sounded and the world collapsed around him.

Mayo spent the rest of the day cramped up over his desk, sifting through the reports, going back over the evidence, and when eventually, at nigh on midnight, he was ready to call it a day, he decided to stretch his legs and expand his mind and lungs with a brisk walk home. He could leave the car in the car park and walk back again in the morning, thereby doubling the benefits. It was a goodish way, through the town and up to the summit of the hill where his flat was situated, although worth it when you got there for the view from his top-floor window, right across the town and the opposite hills beyond. But tonight, instead of going straight home to be met by the companionable ticking of his clocks—seven at the last count, with another spread out in the process of repair, which would make eight if he could find room for it—he found his long strides taking him in the opposite direction, through the meanly terraced streets and back alleys that made up the lower town.

Any passing police patrol would have recognised him; they were used to coming across him at all hours by now. It was a thing he'd begun when he was new to Lavenstock, prowling the night streets like a tom cat, staking out his territory, getting to know it, until now every nook and cranny was as familiar to him as the map of his own face.

Here, where he walked now, small factories and dwelling houses and the occasional corner shop run by Asians existed cheek by jowl. Back entries and closed factory gates interrupted the rows of grimy houses. Some of the areas were scheduled for demolition and there were gaps in the streets that showed backyards and neglected garden plots and vacant lots. Dustbins stood on the kerbside and a forsaken air of dereliction prevailed, though here and there was the occasional house with shining windows and bricks painted in colours to bring back reminders of Caribbean sunshine. In the distance the gaunt tower blocks of the Somerville Estate—contemporary successors of the old brick mill chimneys—rose dark and black, punctured here and there with the floating golden squares of lighted windows, indicating the presence of other night birds like himself.

Leaving the canal behind him, he turned sharply, leaning into the cold east wind and crossing the bridge over the river and on to Stockwell Street and the beginnings of the smarter part of the town. For the second time that day Mayo found himself outside the Community Centre. It stood in darkness, now closed, its bulky presence dwarfing the row of small shops and the wine bar next to it, also shut.

Darkness at the back of the building too, except for one small, dim night-lamp that lit the narrow cantilevered terrace jutting out over the river, where on clement summer evenings a few tables and chairs were set out for drinks. He climbed the half-dozen steps to the terrace, resting his elbows on the railings and looking out over the water. The river flowed swiftly, darkly; the sound of the weir came like distant music. *Did* death come peacefully by drowning? Who could know, except the dead? Ashleigh Cockayne, for instance. Impatiently, symbolically rejecting an idea that he was afraid might easily become an obsession, he turned his back on the dark water and leaned against the railings, facing the theatre.

All was tidy now at the back of the building. Ron Prosser had evidently finished his work, his building tackle had been taken away, so Lili Anand would have something to be pleased about, at any rate. There was nothing now to be seen except a rough scaly patch in one corner where cement had been mixed. The dim light shone on the water-steps where boats could tie up. He fancied for a moment he saw something which stirred the glimmerings of an idea in his mind, an idea which grew, exciting him. No, it wouldn't work, not single-handed. Or would it? He walked down the steps of the terrace and onto the walkway alongside the river, towards the water-steps, and once there got down on his knees. He stood up and thought about it for a long time. The idea, bizarre as it seemed, wouldn't go away.

"Beware of applying logic and common sense to a situation where logic and common sense don't exist," a senior colleague had told him once when he was a very young P.C. And he'd been right. Neither quality had got them very far in this case up to the moment, where neither quality seemed to apply. Right, then. Maybe it was time to see what a bit of intuition and gut feeling could do . . .

ELEVEN

"So here's an undertaking well accomplished!"

THE LOCAL WEEKLY PAPER, the *Advertiser,* came out on Friday, but it was Monday morning before Kite got around to seeing it. He buried his head in it over breakfast while all around him seethed the usual commotion of his family getting ready for the day.

"Mum, you haven't done it yet!" came in an accusing voice from Davey.

Sheila said, "Now, Davey," and grabbed a piece of toast on her way to the bottom of the stairs. "Hurry *up,* Daniel!" she yelled. "Mrs. Barlow'll be here in a couple of minutes." She was still in her dressing gown but her face was made up, her curly brown hair brushed and combed so that she'd be ready to leave for the office in ten minutes flat after the boys had left.

"I can't find my swimming things," Daniel wailed back.

Sheila raced up the stairs. It wasn't her turn to ferry the neighbourhood children to school, or she'd have made Daniel look for them, but as it was it was quicker to go and look herself.

Davey was whingeing on, "Dad, she hasn't written my note yet!"

Kite lowered his paper. "What's the matter with your tie?" he asked, seeing one end somewhere near Davey's right ear, the other by his left knee.

"It doesn't fit me."

"Doesn't *what?* Here, let's have a look." Kite grinned and re-tied the offending garment. "Hopeless, you are, my lad, did you know? And what's all this about a note?"

"For not doing my homework yesterday."

"Oh? And *why* didn't you do your homework yesterday?"

"I was sick."

"You don't look sick to me."

"I'm not now."

Kite regarded the insouciant face of his son and sighed. "Pass me that pad. Is there a pen anywhere?"

"Thanks, Dad, that's brilliant," Davey beamed, while Kite scribbled the note, reproaching himself, not for the first time, for being so little involved in his kids' lives that he didn't even know when they'd been sick. A motor horn sounded outside, there was a last-minute scramble before the boys at last were off, Sheila came back and began to clear the table around him. Kite put his paper down again.

"Leave that, love, I'll do it. Sit down and finish your coffee."

She perched for a token moment on the edge of the chair and took a gulp of coffee before jumping up again. "Must get ready."

"I wrote Davey's note."

"Oh, you did, did you?" she said, pausing. "And you the great detective! Don't you recognise a malingerer when you see one? I told him he'd have to confess to Mrs. Pound himself, Martin."

In that case, Kite was rather glad he'd saved his son an ordeal he wouldn't have wanted to face himself. But in all honesty he had to admit he'd maybe given in too easily. It wasn't an attitude Mrs. Pound herself would have called "supportive." He was a rotten parent, he told himself, and Sheila often had more than her share to put up with, though she rarely complained. "I'm sorry, love." He reached for her hand, drew her down and gave her a kiss. "All the same, I wouldn't wish one of Jennifer Pound's 'little talks' on my worst enemy."

"Oh, you're as bad as Davey!" Sheila said, but he saw he was forgiven. Passing his chair, she bent and rested her cheek briefly on his head. "Bye, love. You'll be gone when I get down, I expect." The headlines on the paper he'd put down stared up at her. "Poor Georgina. What a ghastly thing, Martin."

The murder was, of course, splashed all over the front page. Kite said, "You know Georgina Fleming?"

"Knew her at school, only she was Georgina Culver then."

"You never told me."

"Yes, I did, the other day at breakfast, only you weren't listening."

"How can anybody listen to anything in this morning madhouse?"

Kite demanded. "What was she like then? She's a pretty cool character now."

"Martin Kite, do you seriously think I can sit down, *now* at ten
past eight, oh God, nearly twenty past, and discuss something
you've had plenty of opportunity to ask about before? I've a job to
go to, remember? Not one whose hours I can change to suit myself.
Sorry, must go and dress. Talk to you about it tonight—if you're
in."

Kite's attitude, when Mayo told him of the theory he'd formu-
lated at the back of the Gaiety the previous night, was frankly sceptical, though he didn't actually say so, and he left willingly enough to
see Ron Prosser (Lavenstock) Ltd. Albeit with an air of "well, you're
the boss!" about him.

Prosser's yard proved to be a space at the side of his house, which
was a between-the-wars brick-built semi, the end one of three pairs
wedged in between a terrace of Edwardian stucco and a new shopping parade. A dish aerial for Sky Television was set on the house
roof; the latest Volvo stood on a short concrete drive. It was another windy day and over the back-garden fence Kite could see washing blowing on the line. Pushing open a pair of double wooden
gates with Prosser's name painted across them, he picked his way
across a lunar landscape of heaped red sand, used bricks and piles of
reclaimed timber. A chipped enamel bath lay on its side, several
battered stainless steel sinks propped against it. Steel scaffolding
pipes lay about to trip the unwary, and under a corrugated roof rolls
of wire netting, roofing felt and cement in bags were untidily
housed. Skirting a cement mixer, standing like some asteroid about
to stride forward, Kite made for the office, ramshackle affair in the
corner, with Prosser's pick-up truck outside. As he approached, a
Rottweiller appeared from nowhere and, making no sound, walked
alongside him with the sleek heavy grace of a prize-fighter, sidling
inside with him when he obeyed the instructions to open the door
and enter.

The small room was so cluttered with an old-fashioned safe, a
battered desk and filing cabinets that there was scarcely room to get
inside. Samples of building materials stood around on every surface,

including the floor. The temperature was tropical from an electric fire turned up to full blast, and heavy with smoke from the latest cigarettes of the three occupants—a woman clerk, Prosser himself and the peroxided Jason.

"Seen you somewhere before, haven't I, squire?" Prosser greeted Kite, and before he could answer, "What can I do you for?"

"Police," Kite said, and Prosser raised his eyebrows.

"Oh, so you've finally got round to doing summat about me complaint, then?"

"Coffee, m'duck?" the woman enquired of Kite. "Kettle's just boiled."

"If it's not too much trouble, thanks."

Crossing to a corner where an electric kettle stood on a shelf, she spooned coffee granules and dried milk powder into a generous-sized mug, added hot water and, without asking, three spoonfuls of sugar from a bag. She was of generous proportions herself, big and comfortable, with Dame Edna spectacles and an easy smile. Kite accepted the coffee from her and sipped, trying to ignore the undissolved milk particles. Leaning against the desk, there being no vacant seat, he slipped his hand into his pocket for his notebook and looked for a space on the desk to put the mug while keeping a wary eye on the dog.

"Careful of the Amstrad," Prosser said, "but you don't have to bother none about the dog. Soft as a boiled swede, he is. Wouldn't harm nobody, would you Fritz?"

"Only if he smells bad meat," Jason put in, sniggering at his own unfunny joke.

"Watch your lip, lad," Kite returned, without looking at him. "Mr. Prosser, about those things of yours that went missing. Could you give me a few more details?"

"How many more times do I have to go through it? I already told your lot when I reported it."

"So tell me again. I only want confirmation. What day and so forth."

Prosser assumed an air of resignation. "When was it, Noreen?"

Noreen said promptly, "Over the weekend when they took the

ladder, Tuesday morning when you found the roofing felt and the gas bottle'd gone, wasn't it?"

"That's right, one after t'other. I reported me ladder missing Monday morning to that there Cockayne. Did he care? Not bleedin' likely! There's that gate round to the back as should be kept locked but never is, and when I told him so he said I should take me tackle home every night, silly sod. We had a big argument about it but I wasn't having no Jessie like him telling me what to do, so I jacked it in for a day or two. Tell you the truth, I thought stuff it, if you're not bothered about locking up, why should I sweat me guts out finishing your piddling little roof job? I'd somebody breathing down me neck to do a garridge job and we went on to that. Somebody what pays prompt, not like the bleedin' Council, six months later."

"That's his problem, see," Noreen intervened, when he stopped for breath. "Too blessed independent, always was."

Prosser said, "One-man business like I am—well, one man and a lad, not forgetting the wife here, you might say—I can't afford *not* to be. I have me expenses—you have to keep up with the times or you get left behind." His wide gesture was appropriate for the brand-new word processor on the desk, but nothing else in the office that Kite could see.

"What size of gas bottle was it, Mr. Prosser?"

"Same size as them out there."

"Pretty heavy to handle, by the looks of them."

"One man can manage easy, if he goes about it the right way."

"Let's have a look at 'em more closely, d'you mind?"

They got to work and within half an hour Kite, having decided that he had time to make another call before lunch, was back in the town centre, walking down the street in the older, lower part of the town where T. H. Perryman's, the gent's outfitters, still plied their trade. It wasn't a shop much patronised by Kite. To him a suit was a suit was a suit, to be picked up from a chain store when you had the time. His father, on the other hand, was a regular customer of Per-ryman's, forever going on about how they'd supplied him with his first school blazer fifty years ago, and how he still went there to be measured for all his suits. It was that sort of place.

This was where Greg Foster, he who played de Flores in *The Changeling,* worked. More specifically, where he ran the business for his father-in-law, the present Thomas Perryman, in the confident expectation that it would in due season fall like a ripe plum into his ready and waiting hands.

He'd just finished a tasteful and cunning arrangement of goods in the window, whereby the male population of Lavenstock could, when reluctantly buying that new shirt the wife insisted they needed, see by happy chance the correctly matching tie, slacks and sweater displayed with it and be persuaded into buying the lot. Hey presto, no sweat! No disastrous colour combinations that would send the wife into giggles, and all good business for Perryman's. Greg himself never had any trouble with his clothes, but a lot of his customers were clueless about that sort of thing. He always knew what to wear and when and how, that he must avoid pink shirts like the plague with his reddish brown hair, and how to hide that teeny-weeny tummy bulge which had just begun to appear. It was an instinct. Thoughtfully, he placed a pair of polished olivewood cufflinks in a box on top of the sweater and stood back to admire the effect.

It was then that he noticed the police sergeant who'd been down at the Gaiety on Saturday with his hand on the shop door and knew that Fleming was still haunting him.

"All right, Sandy," he said to his young assistant, "you can get off for your lunch now. Take an extra hour. You did very well deputising for me on Saturday afternoon. Jacket? Of course, sir."

As he showed Kite the rail where a selection of jackets hung Greg relaxed, realising he might have a genuine customer after all, while Kite flicked through them, thinking they all looked very much the same, until he came to one which was very different from the rest. It appeared to him identical with that which Fleming had worn, only this one was in tan suede, not grey, as his had been. It gave him the opening he needed. "Nice quality," he began.

"I can see you have very good taste," Foster said, so Kite knew it would be expensive. But two hundred and forty-five quid! Even allowing for inflation. His last suit had cost just over a hundred and he'd thought that was going over the top.

"They come from Italy," Foster explained reverentially, sliding the jacket off the hanger and holding it out. "We've only had two. The other one—" He stopped in some confusion, remembering to whom the other one had been sold.

"That's all right, sir, I know who bought the other one," Kite said, producing his warrant card. "I'm here to ask you about him."

Greg evidently thought that was a dirty trick. Huffily, he put the jacket back, but he wasn't the sort to stay on his high horse for long. He was naturally friendly and loquacious and genuinely wanted to be helpful.

"Thought I'd seen you somewhere before. I suppose you want to talk to me about Rupert Fleming? It wasn't him who bought the jacket, incidentally, it was his wife. A present, she said. I wonder if she'd have been quite so generous if she'd known about the others."

"The others?"

"The other women . . . or perhaps I shouldn't have said that." Greg shrugged. "Oh, why not, it's no use pretending, because somebody's been talking, haven't they? Somebody's told you I hated his guts? And so I did, along with a lot more people, for different reasons. It'd be hard to find anybody who *liked* him."

"Everybody has somebody, somewhere, they say."

"Not Fleming! Oh all right, I know he's dead and all that blah . . . well, be damned to that, I detested him."

"Any particular reason?"

"Not one reason, dozens. I suppose it started when he gave me a bad notice in that crummy entertainment review column he wrote in the *Advertiser*—not a by-line, just his initials—and okay, I won't deny there might have been some justification for what he wrote that first time. It wasn't the right part for me, but I took it because it was the biggest role I'd been offered so far and I did the best I could with it. He wrote what he did to pay me back and I'm not about to bore you with the exact details—enough to say that he was always clever with words and he made me an absolute laughing-stock. I can take criticism as much as the next person, but that was *annihilating!* I realized my mistake afterwards. I should have ignored the whole thing, pretended I'd never even seen the notice, but it was bloody unfair and I taxed him with it. Which was playing into his hands, because I could guarantee after that he'd do his best to make some

snide, adverse comment about me every time we put a play on.
Though he couldn't go *too* far, folks aren't that simple. I may not be
the world's greatest actor, but I'm not bad, not for Lavenstock,
anyway. And he was rubbish."

Having got that off his chest, he paused to draw breath. Greg
Foster on the face of it seemed harmless enough, but in Kite's experience any man willing to think of another as rubbish was a man to be
watched, so he asked, "What was that you said about paying you
back?"

Foster reddened, with embarrassment it seemed. "Did I say that?
Oh, pay me out for not taking what he said lying down, I suppose I
meant."

"Sure that's what you meant?"

Foster sighed. "No. Not really. The thing is, it's a bit embarrass-
ing. He asked me if I wanted to make a bit of cash on the side—to
be frank, he asked me if I'd ever done any modelling."

"Modelling? Clothes and things, like in the adverts?" Kite asked
innocently, thinking he could well understand why Fleming had
approached Foster, with his smooth photogenic good looks, his
perfect teeth and athletic body.

"No, Sergeant, *not* like in the adverts, and *certainly* not in
clothes," Foster replied shortly. "Like taking them off and being
photographed. I told him what he could do with his photographs.
I'm a married man with two children and another on the way. I'm
not into that sort of thing." He paused before adding carefully,
"Not everybody feels like I do, of course."

"Other members of the cast?"

"Oh, I don't know about that, no, I'm talking about the chap
who came to the Gaiety last week, the week before last, I mean, the
Wednesday before the murder."

"What man was this?"

"I didn't actually see him, but I overheard a conversation between
Fleming and Ashleigh Cockayne, in the men's room. Fleming was
telling Cockayne there was someone asking to see him, Cockayne
was saying he hadn't time to be bothered. 'He has a proposition to
put to us, about you know what,' Fleming said. That was what made
me prick up my ears. 'I think you'll be very interested when you hear

what it is.' And Cockayne said, 'Who's been letting the cat out of the bag?' But he didn't sound too put out, in fact he laughed, and off he went with Fleming, cutting the rehearsal short."

"Wednesday night, you said?" Foster nodded. Wednesday was the night Lili thought Cockayne had begun his row with Fleming. "You've no idea who this man was?"

Foster shook his head and Kite, closing his notebook, thanked him for his cooperation.

"I don't know about cooperation, I've been giving you a pretty good motive for having murdered him myself, haven't I?" Foster gave a short laugh. "I shouldn't pursue that idea if I were you. I wouldn't have risked messing my life up just to get even with a crumb like that. But one thing's for sure, I wasn't a bit surprised when I heard somebody *had* done for him. Frankly, Fleming was a disaster looking for somewhere to happen. He went about deliberately stirring it up. Well, he seemed to *expect* people not to like him. He went in head first, looking for trouble, even when it wasn't there. Ever met people like that?"

"All the time," Kite said. "And they nearly always end up finding it, one way or another."

Mayo heard Kite out and sat so long staring down at his desk with a preoccupied air that Kite was at last moved to say, "What next?" in order to remind him that he was still there.

"Get Underwood up here to the station. I want another word with him."

When the caretaker was sitting before him, supplied with tea, he said, "Cast your mind back to last Wednesday week, Mr. Underwood. Do you remember anyone calling at the Gaiety after the rehearsal, asking to see Mr. Cockayne?"

"No," said Underwood with absolute conviction.

"Or Mr. Fleming?"

"No."

Mayo wasn't satisfied with this. It seemed unlikely that anybody enquiring for Cockayne would have got past Underwood without his knowing, and yet he had the impression the caretaker was telling the truth. Another possibility existed—that Underwood himself was the man Fleming had been referring to; in the oblique sort of way someone might say "a man about a dog" he'd said "a man with a proposition." Cockayne may have laughed, getting the implication, but any proposition Underwood was likely to make would almost certainly have been blackmail.

But there was nothing he could do to shift Underwood from the stance he'd taken up, and for the moment he was obliged to accept his statement.

TWELVE

"There's horror in my service, blood and danger."

DOWN BY THE RIVER, it was as cold as charity. The day which had started so brilliantly, in such clear sunshine, had become raw and grey, the wind blowing in fierce gusts. It seemed as if it might rain. In the face of the outright scepticism of most of those gathered there, Mayo's convictions no longer seemed quite so clear-cut as last night. Paradoxically, this resolved his doubts.

Yes, he told himself, it could have been done that way. Cockayne *could* have lashed himself to the gas bottle and rolled himself into the river. It was quite conceivable. Far stranger and more macabre things had been known. To a mind bent on suicide, anything was possible.

And there was no turning back now in any case. The back entrance to the Gaiety had been sealed off to all but police vehicles and those belonging to the sub-aqua team. As a starting point, Mayo had pointed out the place where he had first noticed the marks where something heavy appeared to have been dragged fairly recently over the stone flags above the water-steps. There were two divers, who had adjusted their masks, slipped nonchalantly into the murky water at the edges and disappeared. Lifting gear was standing by. The team of detectives stamped their feet and waited.

They didn't have long to wait. With a sense of half-restrained horror they stood by as the thing was hauled up and broke the surface of the water. A long cylindrical shape, black and obscene, sagging in the middle. And then there was a collective release of held breath when it was seen that what had been brought up was Prosser's missing roll of roofing felt, bound around with wire. Perhaps it had been thrown into the river by vandals, maybe the ladder and the gas bottle too. The operation started again.

This time, the divers seemed to stay down below an unconscionable length of time. After a while Mayo went up the steps and onto the upper terrace, thinking he might see better what was going on from there, but no sooner had he put his foot on the top step than there was a shout from Kite.

Immediately the group below sprang into action again to get the lifting gear lowered to the men below the water. Mayo was about to descend and join them when a hand clutched his arm. "What's happening?"

He turned to see the small, black-clad figure of Lili Anand. Behind her was the open door into the theatre bar, which he had ordered to be kept locked until the operation was over, though doubtless she had her own key. "Go back inside, Lili, please," he told her sharply.

"It's Ashleigh, isn't it? You're looking for Ashleigh." She had begun to shiver uncontrollably. She looked shrunken, and old underneath the mask of her heavy make-up. "I knew it. I saw it, a body in the water . . ."

"This is no place for you at the moment."

He thought she was going to break away from him and run down to the water's edge, all the same. Cursing the inopportuneness of her arrival, he grasped her arm firmly and looked around for someone to deal with her, but everyone else seemed to be occupied. Keeping his grasp on her arm, he began to hurry her back into the theatre, in through the open door again. Rather to his surprise, she made no objection. "Do you have a key to the bar?" he asked as they stepped inside. "To get yourself a brandy or something?"

She sank onto one of the plastic chairs. "Please. Don't bother about me. I'll get myself a hot coffee or something. You go back to your duties, I'll stay inside. Don't worry, I've no wish to be there when they . . . when . . ."

"You'll be all right?"

She nodded slowly, as if with a great effort. "You're very kind."

Although by no means satisfied, he was obliged to accept her word. However much he pitied her, he had more important things to occupy himself with than hysterical or distressed females. He nodded doubtfully and went back towards the landing stage, where he was met by Kite, walking towards him like a man who doesn't believe what he's just seen.

"What've they found this time?"

"I think you'd better come and take a look, sir."

The unusual formality as he spoke, the stiff, frozen look on his normally mobile features made Mayo follow him immediately, without comment.

The divers, sleek as seals in their dripping wet-suits, were back on dry land, surrounded by a silent bevy of uniformed and plain-clothes men. What they had found had been brought to the surface and now lay on the ground.

This second body had been anchored down by the heavy gas bottle, all right. But there was no question of suicide. Rather than embracing the cylinder from the front as a man might do to tie himself to it, the body had its back to it, wrists and ankles pulled to the back and securely knotted together behind with a rope which had then been cut short. Another ligature was around his waist, similarly tied. There was a nasty wound on his head.

And the body wasn't that of Ashleigh Cockayne.

It had been in the water for over a week now and would hardly have been recognisable but for the thick mop of fair curly hair, now dark with water.

Never again would P.C. Andrew Mitchell be ribbed as a budding Einstein.

"The heat's on," said Superintendent Howard Cherry, winding up. "I want him found, the bugger who's done this. *Whatever* the reason."

The grim silence of his colleagues, foregathered in his office, told the superintendent his outrage had an echo in every heart, though nobody liked the implications of that "whatever." He'd be found, all right. Found, and duffed up if some of Mitch's mates had their way. They wouldn't be allowed to, of course, that sort of thing never happened, did it? No senior officer would ever turn a blind eye to that sort of thing, would they? Of course not. But Cockayne would wish he'd never been born.

Cockayne? Mayo thought, all his macho instincts to the fore. An actor. A bloody *actor,* with big soft eyes and a lock of hair that fell over his forehead. To bash Mitch over the head with a blow that had killed him, then heave him into the river, lashed to a heavy gas cylinder? Not to mention blowing Rupert Fleming's head off. He must have gone berserk.

"But what did Mitch think he was *doing,* for God's sake?" Cherry went on. "He wasn't C.I.D.—and even if he had been, he'd no business . . . it was totally outwith his responsibilities."

Cherry was shrewd and capable and generally well respected, but he was a man ordained by nature to order and obedience, conditioned by training and advancement to cleave to establishment procedures, suits and haircuts. He ran a tight ship and it offended his strong sense of propriety that one of their number should have stepped out of line. So far out as to go and get himself killed, by being hit on the head with something sharp and heavy, before being thrown into the river, the doctors had said. He didn't like that at all.

"He was a good lad." This was Reader, a sober man who was Mayo's opposite number in the uniformed branch. "Enthusiastic. But a bit impulsive. Had to tear him off a strip more than once for going off at half cock."

"He won't be doing it again," Cherry said, tight-lipped. "That's for sure."

The shock had run through the station like a lighted fuse. Mitch was one of their own, a popular lad with a bright future before him, and well liked by everyone with his jokes and his good-humoured, breezy personality. His murder had left them all raw, a bit touchy. Especially Cherry, who'd started with a suicide enquiry on his hands that had looked fairly straightforward and was now anything but.

A policeman killed in the close proximity of a theatre with which a victim and his suspected murderer had also been involved demanded questions about any connections between them, which was what Cherry's "whatever" was all about. His murder could hardly have come out of the blue. But what sort of connections? There'd been one, at least. Mitch had been aware of the two men's dubious activities. Janet Lindsay had told him.

Poor Janet, nearly out of her mind with shock and horror. "I only mentioned it briefly, what I thought was going on, sir, because I was concerned about young Trish. He warned me to cool it, to keep my eyes and ears open but otherwise do nothing until I was more certain. And then to go and poke about doing something off his own bat . . . it was having spare time on his hands, I suppose. Oh God, if I hadn't gone to Rhodes . . ."

She looked so pale and distraught, so shaken out of her usual unflappable calmness, but Mayo hadn't the heart to tell her not to blame herself. It would be a waste of time because she would anyway, whatever he said. She was going through her own private hell at the moment, but she was tough and sensible; she would come through, given time.

"It was that Oscar thing on his desk. You know the one," Kite announced with barely concealed satisfaction, lowering himself onto the arm of the chair on the far side of Mayo's desk, prepared for a discussion.

Although Mayo's men had previously searched Cockayne's office for any clues as to why he'd gone missing, the forensic team had now been called in and, with a different objective in mind, with Cockayne now chief suspect in two murders, one of which had probably taken place on the premises, their minute searches had met some interesting discoveries. Not least, what was thought to be the murder weapon, which had been standing on Cockayne's desk all the time.

By "Oscar" Kite meant an ostentatious-looking trophy in the form of a bust of George Bernard Shaw, which the Lavenstock Thespians had brought home in triumph that year from a national amateur dramatic festival. It was about twelve inches high, standing on a square base, and the whole thing had been cast in some heavy base metal, then finished in shiny plastic gold. It was too much to hope that it hadn't been wiped clean of fingerprints by the murderer, but protective felt had been stuck under the base to prevent it scratching any polished surface it might stand on, and it was almost certain there would be minute traces of blood and hair, invisible to the naked eye, still adhering to that. The lab would give their verdict as soon as possible—and on some of the vinyl floor tiles which had been removed for examination also—but Doc Ison was of the opinion anyway that the corner of the base would definitely correspond with the wound on the temple. The post mortem had revealed a *contre-coup* injury on the back of the head, showing that Mitch had fallen, or been pushed, onto some hard surface, probably the floor, before the fatal blow to the temple had been delivered.

The use of the trophy as the murder weapon positively linked Mitch's murder with Cockayne, if anything more had been needed.

"Obviously left there because Cockayne knew it would be missed if he got rid of it," Mayo surmised. "Sort of makes its presence felt, a thing like that. You'd be bound to notice if it wasn't there."

"Lili Anand certainly would. She told Spalding she puts it back on the desk every morning because Underwood always moves it to what he considers a better place when he cleans the office."

"That figures!"

"That conversation Foster overheard in the men's room—it must've been Mitch they were talking about," Kite said. "He must've gone down there that night after the rehearsal to have a look for himself after Lindsay told him what she suspected . . . he taxed them with it . . . Cockayne killed him . . . they slung him in the river and that was it."

Mayo, leaning back in his chair, contemplating the ceiling, brought his gaze back to Kite's face. "Let's not go over the top on this, Martin. You're assuming too much where we can't afford to assume one damn thing. Mitch *might* have gone down there. Cockayne *might* have killed him. All right, suppose Mitch *had* found out what was going on, suppose he had proof even—though how the hell he could've had is beyond me at the moment—they'd be in it over the ears all right, but killing a police officer . . . hardly likely to make things any better, was it?"

"You know what they're like, some of these types. Land out first, think after."

"He was a big lad. He knew how to take care of himself."

"There were two of them, for Christ's sake!"

"Okay, okay—"

"They'd have got the wind up when they realized what they'd done, what a helluva stir a missing copper was going to make—or Fleming did, and maybe threatened to blow it—and so Cockayne decided to finish him off too, setting it up to look like suicide."

"It's a theory." Mayo sprang to his feet and began to pace restlessly. "But we haven't one scrap of evidence that that was how it happened. I realize it's an emotive subject, Mitch being concerned and all, but for God's sake let's keep an open mind, Martin. We don't *know* he went down to the theatre to confront them. If we don't go putting our own interpretation on what Greg Foster overheard, we can get a very different picture."

Kite stiffened. "You're saying that *Mitch* was trying to get a nice little line going with those bastards! It's what the super thinks as well, isn't it?"

"Don't put words into my mouth. I'm saying nothing, except that it's dangerous to make your mind up and then look for the evidence to support what you think. In my own mind I can't believe any such thing about Mitch, I tell myself he couldn't possibly be involved in muck like that—but it happens. And when the time comes that we can build a case on gut feeling alone, you let me know."

Kite sat rigid, every pore giving out signals of outrage and disbelief.

"Mind you," Mayo went on, "off the record, I'm not going to say you could be wholly wrong."

Nobody on the whole strength envied George Atkins the job he was sent out to do, least of all Kite, who was sent with him, dragging his feet like an unwilling schoolboy, feeling like every kind of a heel.

Atkins, staid and unflappable, with half a lifetime's experience, twenty years of that in C.I.D., was more philosophical. Though disliking what they had to do no less than Kite, he knew it wasn't the first time a copper had been suspected of being bent and it wouldn't be the last. He was prepared to reserve judgement.

Mitch had lived on his own in what was grandly termed a flat but was in reality no more than a superior bed-sitter with an alcove off forming a tiny but well-designed kitchen, equipped with what Kite recognised as do-it-yourself units. The pot plants were still thriving, there was food in the fridge: a portion of pork pie that was by now rather suspect, half a bottle of white wine, some tomatoes and cheese and the heart of a slightly wilted lettuce. The only thing missing was Mitch.

His landlady was stunned with the news. She said, "Well, I don't know, he came home last week and said he'd had a good holiday. I haven't seen him since last Wednesday, but there was times when I didn't see him for weeks, his job being what it is."

Mrs. Ainstey was a young mother with three under-school-age children, which prevented her from going out to work, and that was why, when the mortgage rates went up again, she and her husband had decided to let the front room, to help out with the finances. Over a cup of tea in the kitchen, with the children shunting cars round their feet, she said, "We talked it over a lot—I mean, letting strangers into your home, it can be asking for trouble, can't it? But Mitch was a real nice guy, helped my Dave put the kitchen units in there he did, papered and painted it all afterwards, him and his girlfriend. Wouldn't have surprised me if he hadn't moved out soon, though. I mean, it wouldn't have mattered to me if she'd moved in with him, I'm not narrow-minded, but there's not much room for two in there, is there? Not on a permanent basis."

Kite hadn't expected Mitch's quarters to be especially tidy but they were as spruce as the corner of a barrack room, the divan bed neatly restored to its daytime use, and glancing round he was surprised to find how well organised and comfortable the small space was. One wall was completely filled with unit shelves that accommodated more books than Kite owned, many of them law books. So poor old Mitch hadn't been kidding about that degree, he'd really been serious. Life was a bit of a bugger, sometimes.

Well okay, that was the easy part. Now for the other.

You couldn't get much lower, Kite reflected, than going through your mate's private belongings, his bank books and insurances, valuing his suits, his shoes, even his Marks and Sparks shirts and underwear.

"What are we expected to find, for God's sake?" he muttered. "Savile Row suits and a bank balance to match the Aga Khan's? They'll be lucky."

"Just keep on looking, son," said Atkins, unflappably. "As if he was any other murder victim. That's all we're here for, for now."

"All right, George, all right, I know what we have to do. But I just don't have to like it as well, okay?"

Kite was relieved, though in actual fact he knew it proved nothing, that the only evidence of wealth they could find was a Building Society account book with small amounts thriftily stashed in it month by month. And the only extravagance a fairly extensive music centre and a couple of deep, comfortable armchairs—the sort of stuff you might invest in to make a good start to a married life, which was probably what it, and the bank account, were intended for. Mitch had made no secret to anybody what he felt about Janet Lindsay.

And then Atkins found his personal diary. And so much for Cherry's "whatever" and whatever nasty suspicions he might have had about what Mitch was up to.

THIRTEEN

"When the deed's done,
I'll furnish thee with all things for thy flight;
Thou may'st live bravely in another country."

THEY MET IN THE CORRIDOR, their paths crossing as Mayo
came into the building and Alex, looking pale and fagged out, left to
go off duty. "We're becoming like ships that pass in the night. Time
something was done about it," Mayo remarked, hearing its triteness
and thinking that Kite would no doubt have found something flip or
amusing to make her laugh, but his own brand of humour was of a
different sort.

She smiled anyway and the tiredness left her face. "I know," she
said. "In fact, I've been trying to reach you all afternoon. Lois is
coming round tonight for supper. Nothing special. We'd both like
to see you, but I don't suppose there's the faintest chance of your
making it?"

"Not a hope in hell, love, I'm sorry."

"Oh, well."

She wouldn't have asked him without good reason, knowing as
she did what the situation was, how impossible it was for him to get
away for any sort of social interchange just now. He guessed she'd
suggested the meeting for his sake as well as her sister's. Knowing
that Lois was sometimes hostile towards him, she was thinking it
would make things easier for both of them if they met on neutral
ground. He doubted it. It was never a good idea for personal relationships to intrude into an investigation. On the other hand, he
was investigating the case and if Lois was willing to talk to him, if
she had something to say that might help, then perhaps he'd better
accept the offer on her own terms, rather than have to question her
as an unwilling witness. And besides—he needed breathing space in
the middle of all this mess; he was still savage about the loss of

Mitch, a good man whose death had been unnecessary. An hour off, helping to get it all in perspective, might not be the worst idea he'd had in months.

"Tell you what—I'll pop in round about half nine. Don't wait supper for me, a coffee and sandwich'll suit me fine. We should be able to wrap things up for tonight by then—unless anything else crops up meantime. Best I can do, I'm afraid, and don't bank on it."

She knew better than that. "It's more than I expected in the circumstances," she smiled. "I'll get off, then." But she didn't go. "Gil, I heard the latest about Mitch. They found his diary, I gather?"

"That's right." Mayo all of a sudden felt happier, remembering that. He didn't give a damn for Cherry's reasons for wanting the young constable cleared—or not much, anyway. He was just glad the lad's notes had proved he wasn't bent, only that he'd been a damn fool. Either you kept broadly to the rules in this outfit or you got out, and Mitch should've known it. There were no medals for doing your own thing. Policing wasn't a profession for heroes or kudos seekers. But he hadn't deserved to die just because he'd forgotten that.

The two women had had seafood for supper and Alex had made him sandwiches of prawns in brown bread, which were good, very good indeed, carefully made and perfectly served, just as the meal would have been. Alex's attitude to food wasn't adventurous or imaginative like his daughter Julie's was, but then, she wasn't intending making a career out of cooking and what she lacked in originality she made up for in excellence.

Afterwards he sat back with his coffee, relaxed and easy as he'd learned to be in Alex's cool, neutral room. It had intimidated him once, just as she had. He'd thought once that nobody could ever live up to her fastidious standards, and to a certain extent he still did. It sounded a note of caution which he now occasionally listened to whenever he was tempted to push his luck and try to persuade her yet again to marry him.

As he watched her sitting with her long legs curled under her in a corner of the sofa, for the first time that day he felt right with himself, the way he always did when he was with her. In off-duty dark red sweater and full skirt, she had a rounded softness that was only hinted at when she was in uniform, but there was still that neat coordination he liked so much in her, what he could only think of as a relaxed precision, that contrasted favourably with the sharp brittleness of her sister. And yet it was Alex who was the tough one. Not simply tough in the way a policewoman had to be, but essentially unbreakable.

Lois, now . . .

From where he was sitting, he could see her face reflected in the glass, looking oddly different as faces do in a mirror. There was a brilliance about her, a shine to her eyes that he might have put down to fever had he not remembered she wore contact lenses. She had several flashing rings on her fingers and a big glittering paste brooch on her lapel, none of them pretending to be real, and he felt she might jangle if she moved, as if she were made of glass prisms. The shimmering image in the mirror made her look both unreal and uncertain, quite unlike the elegant, assured Lois he was used to. He felt suddenly sorry for her and the sharp unreal way of life to which she was committed, and turning away from the reflection to face the real Lois, he approached the matter of Rupert Fleming more obliquely than he felt naturally disposed to.

She blinked several times, as if needing to get him and what he was saying into focus. With a nervous laugh, she said, "There's no need to beat about the bush, please. I know you're dying to know."

"What do you know I'm dying to know?"

"About me—and Rupert."

He sat back, put his hands behind his head and stretched his legs. "All right, what are you prepared to tell me?"

She asked abruptly, "What time was he killed?"

"Difficult to say," he answered, feeling as cagey and uncommunicative as Doc Ison. "Some time around midnight on Monday evening, we think."

"He came to see me on Monday night."

He sat up. "What time?"

"Half past nine. The news and weather forecast had just finished and I was debating whether to watch the next programme or have an early night when I heard the bell to the flat ringing. He must have been leaning on it and it rang and rang until I answered. It was very frightening, the way it went on and on like that. Terrifying, actually. I don't get many visitors that time of night."

He didn't think she was overstating the case. Her face had paled at the remembered moment. Her cup rattled alarmingly on its saucer and Alex took it from her. Forestalling criticism, she went on hastily, "Yes, I did ask who it was before I opened the door. But I almost wished I hadn't opened it when I saw him."

"Had he been drinking?"

"No, no. He was stone-cold sober. He never drank much, anyway. But he was in a state . . . sort of wild and unbalanced. I'd never seen him like that before. He pushed past me and ran up the stairs. I asked him just what he thought he was doing and then— then he said he'd come to ask me to lend him some money."

She began to fiddle with one of the flashing rings on her fingers, avoiding his eye. He caught Alex's carefully non-committal expression and knew that she was thinking the same as he was, that it was probably by no means the first time this had happened. She rushed on, with slightly heightened colour, "Naturally I asked him what he wanted it for, but he wouldn't say. And of course, I hadn't any, not the amount he wanted, not even in the till, because people usually pay me by cheque or credit card. I told him my cash was all tied up and that I'd get some the following day if it was that important, but he said that'd be too late. I gave him thirty pounds, which was all I had. Apparently it wasn't enough."

"Not enough for what? Did he say why he wanted it?"

She shook her head and hesitated before continuing, looking at Alex as she spoke. "He began to go round the room, picking things up and stuffing them in his pockets, the snuff boxes and scent bottles, that old silver photoframe of Aunt Em's, my old china—what he called 'nice disposable assets.' I could hardly believe it possible and of course I tried to stop him, but not too hard, I must admit, I was too frightened. He seemed to me a man at the end of his tether, as if he might tip over the edge. I told him to stop it. I think I said, 'This is something you'll regret later,' or something like that, and he said, 'Probably. It isn't a thing I usually do, darling, my friends' teaspoons are usually safe with me, but needs must when the devil

drives. One day I'll pay you back.' There were too many things for
his pockets so he took them out and asked for a bag to carry them
and the bigger stuff in. I only had a Harrods one. He laughed like
mad when he saw it. 'Oh, very appropriate,' he said, 'very Lois!' But
it wasn't, all those delicate things jumbled together in the bottom of
a plastic bag, without any protection."

It was the sort of ironic joke it amused Lois to tell against herself,
in other circumstances. Now she wasn't even faintly amused. Nor
was Alex. "I thought your room looked bare," was all she said.

"Because the next day I cleared everything else away too, so you
wouldn't notice the missing things, my love. What was left looked
so stupid, somehow, on their own, just dotted about. Well . . . it
was quite a haul he got away with."

"In money terms, how much?"

"Actually, about six and a half thousand, in all," she answered
after a pause.

"Six and a half !"

"They're mostly what I've picked up at sales, over the years," she
said defensively. "And I don't suppose I'll ever get them back, but
I've got records if you want to see them. And photographs, too. I'm
prepared now because I've been burgled a couple of times before
. . . but never by someone I—oh God, I just feel so *sick* when I
think of it."

Alex murmured comforting things. Mayo said nothing. Questions
were piling up in his brain. Why had Fleming come to *Lois* for
money? Why hadn't he borrowed from Georgina? Why had he
needed it? Was it to pay off Cockayne, who'd maybe been trying a
spot of blackmail, because he knew it was Fleming who'd killed
Mitch? Or had he been going to make a bid to get away from Cockayne, for the same reason? But if so, why had he then gone on to the
theatre, and once there, why had Cockayne plied him with the
spiked whisky, driven him to Scotley Beeches, where he'd shot him
and then made off, presumably with the valuables Fleming had
stolen and the thirty pounds Lois had given him?

It made no sense. God dammit, nothing made sense, this case was
getting on his nerves! It was giving him a bad headache, of the sort

he hadn't had in years. Nothing seemed to look the right way up, as if he were looking at a photograph printed the wrong way round, or Lois's reflection in the glass.

He rubbed his hand across his face, all at once realizing how little sleep he'd had over the last week. But he was used to going without sleep, especially when he was on a case like this. The will to carry on, with just the occasional cat-nap, came from somewhere as long as you kept going along with it. It had been a mistake to stop and relax, he should have known that. But he shouldn't be feeling this rotten. You only got like this when you couldn't cope, he thought in disgust. Symbolic rejection, or something.

"You all right, Gil?" Alex was looking at him with concern.

"Just tired. Bushed, in fact. Think I'll be making tracks."

He'd leave his car and walk home, the brisk night air would revive him and he'd be able to think more clearly. Lois had been telling him something important and he needed to sort it out.

She stood up to leave. "Don't go because of me, I need an early night anyway. No thanks, I have my car," she said to Mayo, wrongly anticipating the offer of a lift. "Good night."

He waited until Alex had seen her sister to the door. He appreciated Lois's somewhat heavy-handed tact, and knew also this was going to be one of the nights he would be invited to stay with Alex, but he doubted if he even wanted to. He knew now, despite his tiredness, that he was in for a sleepless night. Probably fall into bed poleaxed, sleep for a couple of hours and that would be it. Wake in the middle of the night, turning the case over in his mind. Get up to make the inevitable pot of tea. But he had the strongest disinclination to leave his comfortable chair that he'd ever had in his life and when Lois had gone he sank back, bone weary, into it.

He woke during the night with a stiff neck and an excruciating pain in his gut, for a moment wondering where the hell he was, and only just made it to the bathroom before he threw up and lost his prawn sandwiches.

After that, further sleep was impossible. He lay stretched out on the sofa in the living room, waiting to feel less as though someone had kicked him hard with a heavy boot in the midriff. The last time this had happened to him had been on his honeymoon with Lynne, when they'd eaten oysters. The memory was still painful and humiliating enough for him not to want to think of it in relation to his present unhappy state. He thought, but of other things. About what Lois had said. About her distorted reflection and the series of images and discoveries that floated before him. And as if his mind as well as his body had been purged and emptied, and feeling better now that he knew his malaise had a physical cause, some of the answers to much of what had been puzzling him over Rupert Fleming's death became clearer to him.

A reasonably early homecoming, a decent home-cooked meal with two helpings of pudding, the kids in bed and a quiet evening in front of the fire because there was only the usual rubbish on the telly . . . it was Kite's idea of heaven at that particular moment.

"If you're going to go to sleep," Sheila said, switching off another chance to see a situation comedy repeat, "I may as well go and do the ironing."

"Have a heart! What else do you expect after a meal like that, brilliant conversation?"

"After not seeing you all week, it's not unreasonable to expect *something*. After making you that bread-and-butter pudding, against my better judgement. You'll be getting fat, as well as losing your powers of speech."

Kite stretched his skinny length and grinned lazily. "Not bad, that pud. You're learning. Nearly as good as the one my mother used to make."

Sheila aimed a cushion at his head, which he neatly fielded. "No stopping you when it comes to the compliments, is there, my lad? Well, aren't you even going to ask me about Georgina Culver?" she demanded.

Kite sat up, blinking himself properly awake. He'd forgotten all about that. It seemed like a hundred years ago since she'd mentioned it. It wasn't all that important, the fact that Sheila had been at school with Fleming's wife, but it might be useful in giving them some background information on the investigation and he oughtn't to have forgotten it. Anything connected with this screwy case which might throw some light into a dark corner would be welcome.

"What about Georgina Culver, then?"

Sheila hesitated before going on. "Martin, I know you never talk much about your work at home . . ."

"No love, I don't. I come home to unwind," Kite interrupted gently. "I'm hardly ever away from the job as it is, without bringing it home as well."

She smiled. "I know, I'm not getting at you. But I've been thinking," she said. She put another log on the fire, then sat on the hearthrug, hugging her knees, the lamplight shining on her rumpled curly brown hair. Her face needed doing and she looked about sixteen, the age she'd been when Kite had first met her, when she'd ridden her bicycle into the back of his . . . typical of Sheila, if he'd but known it then, who'd been born accident-prone. Spontaneous, warm-hearted, energetic, her progress through life was attended by a series of minor mishaps. Even now, when she'd succeeded in carving out a career for herself in personnel management after the boys were old enough to be less of a tie, there was always something . . . locking herself out of the house, giving a cup of tea and a sandwich to a tramp who then walked off with the electric hedge clippers she'd left out on the lawn . . . setting fire to the *vacuum cleaner* by picking up an unused match, for heaven's sake!

Kite grinned and reached out to the table by his side and held up the coffee pot. Sheila passed her mug and when he'd refilled it, she said, "I suppose you're looking for somebody who might have had a grudge against Rupert Fleming?"

"That's the general idea. Are you suggesting by any chance Georgina Fleming might have had one?"

"I'm hardly qualified to say that! Anyway, she wasn't anyone I knew very well, she was younger than me, further down the school. She was in the netball team for a while when I was captain, though, and I remember her as very sharp and clever. You never knew what she was thinking."

"Things don't change," Kite said feelingly.

"I don't suppose they do. She was always winning prizes, expected to be brilliant at something or other . . . it seemed to surprise everyone when she got engaged so young—apparently the Head was very disappointed. I'd left school then, but I remember hearing about it on the old girls' grapevine."

"But she didn't *marry* Fleming until after she'd finished with college . . . and it hasn't stopped her from making a pretty successful career for herself."

"I'm not talking about Rupert Fleming. I'm talking about Tim Salisbury. She got engaged to him when she was seventeen and they were going to be married. There was talk of her not going to college, even. But she did, and then married Rupert Fleming instead."

"Tim Salisbury? Well, well. Yes, I see where your thoughts are tending. You think *Salisbury* might have been harbouring a grudge against Fleming for pinching his girl. But that's a heck of a long time to bear resentment, and besides, Salisbury's married to someone else —his wife's a very beautiful woman. Anybody married to her isn't likely to be sniffing around elsewhere, take it from me. He's besotted with her. With very good reason, I might say."

"I've heard that on the grapevine too," Sheila responded rather coolly. "But is *she* besotted with him?"

"Ah. You mean Susan Salisbury and Rupert Fleming? And Tim Salisbury murdering Fleming out of jealousy . . . for taking first Georgina, then Susan?" Kite shook his head. "Complicated. And it won't do. That aspect of it—I mean the possibility of Susan Salisbury and Rupert Fleming being connected—it was one of the first things we checked up on. And discounted."

"Oh well, it was just a thought. Silly, really."

"No, it's not, love. I'm glad you mentioned it, but I doubt if it's going to make any difference at this stage."

FOURTEEN

"I could not get the ring without the finger."

MAYO LEARNED NEXT MORNING, with that slight sense of
victimisation and injury of the unfairly afflicted, that although both
Lois and Alex had eaten the shell fish, neither had been affected.
Only one, though, he thought sourly, it needed only one. The one
he'd eaten.

He still felt as though he might, with very great probability, die,
but a day at home at this stage in the investigation, as Alex suggested, wasn't on, not even to be contemplated. Nothing would
have kept him away from his office now, anyway. He went in as soon
as he decently could and told Kite briefly of the new developments,
arranging to discuss them more fully with him later, ignoring the
sergeant's quizzical glance at his whey face. There were still things he
wanted to get clear in his mind which he felt better able to deal with
alone than with Kite hovering sympathetically at his shoulder.

Out of interest, before he left Mayo alone in his office, Kite told
him about his conversation with Sheila the previous evening. "If
we'd known there'd been any connection between Salisbury and
Georgina Fleming in the first place, it might've saved a lot of bother
checking it out, but it's academic now, seeing it's Cockayne we're
after."

Mayo doodled thoughtfully on his scratch pad. "I don't know, I
think I'd still like to have a word with him. He *was* once attached to
Georgina, and maybe we shouldn't ignore that. We haven't got
hands on our murderer yet." He stared down at the papers on his
desk in so preoccupied and concentrated a manner that Kite was
obliged to clear his throat to remind his superior that he was still in
the room. "All right, yes, let's have a talk to friend Salisbury—but
we'll do it here. I don't fancy trying to get anything sensible out of
him while he's got one eye hovering over that wife of his."

He spent the next hour apparently doing nothing, and then sent for his sergeant again, who came in bearing a stack of new reports and said that he'd put out a trace for the items Fleming had stolen, though without much hope of results. They might, or might not, turn up sometime later, but where was anybody's guess. If Cockayne now had them, as seemed likely, he wouldn't have tried to get rid of them until he was well clear of Lavenstock, if he'd any sense, and by now he'd be miles away, his car probably abandoned . . .

Kite broke off and gave Mayo an anxious look. "Excuse my saying so, but wouldn't you be better at home and in bed?"

Mayo saw that Alex had told Kite what had happened, who as a recently recovered invalid himself, and having had the benefit of a good night's sleep, probably felt entitled to be concerned, but Mayo wasn't having any. "No thank you, Martin, I would not be better at home and in bed."

"We can manage for the rest of the day, surely. You look terrible."

"I'm all right, dammit!" Mayo rubbed a hand over his face, then smiled faintly. "As a matter of fact, though I may still look like death warmed up, I'm on top of the world."

"You reckon?" Kite replied sceptically.

"Halfway up Everest, anyway. Look, get hold of Dexter and ask him what the hell he's doing with that fingerprint report—"

"Funny you should ask, he's on his way over with it, he wants to see you."

"Does he? About time, too. Send him up as soon as he arrives. And come in yourself, I think you might find it interesting. Meanwhile, I do believe some hot tea and a bit of toast wouldn't come amiss."

Dexter was a thin man with sparse sandy hair and a misleading air of anxious uncertainty that concealed extreme efficiency and positiveness.

"You've got the report for me? Good, sit down then, Dave."

Dexter placed his little bombshell on Mayo's desk, sat down and waited.

Mayo scanned the report quickly; then he read it again, more slowly. He leaned back and stared at the wall opposite. Then he smiled at Dexter and handed over the report to his sergeant, watched while Kite read. "Well?"

"Hell's bells," said Kite.

"You're sure about this, Dave?" Mayo asked, but only for form's sake.

"Yes," said Dexter.

Dexter was an expert. He could read fingerprints like other people read faces. They believed him without question, without need of the proof positive before them in the shape of the official report complete with diagrams, photographs and the rest, when he said the prints in Cockayne's office and in his home, all over his personal belongings—his papers, his toothbrush and razor—were identical with the fingerprints of the dead man in the car.

"Well," Mayo said.

All feelings of still being vaguely unwell had gone. Some colour had reappeared in his cheeks and excitement lit his eyes, making them silver-grey, like mercury. His thoughts were clocking round at a furious rate. It was not too much to say that he suddenly felt born-again, or at the very least as if he'd spent a week at a health farm. What Dexter said confirmed the conclusions he'd groped towards during the small hours. At last he knew the cause of his own unease with the case. The photograph had appeared to be the wrong way round because he'd been looking at it back to front. The shot victim was Ashleigh Cockayne, not Rupert Fleming. And it might justifiably be assumed, therefore, that it was Fleming who was the murderer, not only of Cockayne, but of Mitch too.

"I need a boot up the backside for not thinking of it before," he admitted to Kite, when Dexter had gone. "There was something that wasn't quite right, something offbeam about this whole set-up, even from the beginning. I've been a blithering idiot not to have seen it before, because I think I had some sort of inkling right from when I picked up that jacket at the scene of the crime."

"What had that to do with it?" Kite asked.

"I ought to have spotted earlier that it didn't belong to the dead man. Whoever he was, he must've been a heavy smoker—his fingers were deeply nicotine-stained, Timpson-Ludgate remarked on it—but the jacket didn't smell of cigarette smoke. It would've reeked if it had belonged to that body. And remember what Bryony Harper said about Fleming being so health-conscious? Is it likely he'd have smoked and run the risk of lung cancer? And I think we shall find that the forensic report will give us a bit more," he went on. "Whoever wore the jacket had been sweating profusely. Not Cockayne's sweat, I'll bet. Nor his hairs on the collar, or his skin flakes on the fabric."

"Fleming," Kite said. "Good grief, yes, it has to be. He of all people would've known how to get hold of Culver's gun . . . and it explains the pills and the booze. They may've been Georgina's pills, ten to one they were, but it wasn't *Fleming* who drank the whisky."

"Right. He was the one who made the suggestion that Cockayne should take young Trish out to look for a taxi to take her home. He'd also suggested a drink to Cockayne—who, one gathers, wouldn't need much persuading—and he'd know where Cockayne kept his whisky. Easy enough then to pour two glasses, while Cockayne was down below, doping one of them, then when Cockayne began to feel drowsy, to suggest driving him home. And instead drive him to Scotley Beeches. Despite what Underwood thought he saw, I'm satisfied Fleming wasn't drunk, only staggering from holding Cockayne up, already woozy. By the time they reached the forest Cockayne would be out for the count. So all Fleming had to do was drag him out of the passenger seat and into the front one, leave his own jacket on the other seat, substitute his own wristwatch and his wallet for Cockayne's, and then shoot him with the gun he'd pinched from Culver, turning Cockayne's head first towards the window. He was shot directly in the face to make sure his features were obliterated to the point where he was virtually unrecognisable. Not possible for anyone to have done this from outside the car if he was sitting facing forward. And of course, the suicide note on the dash would've been left by Fleming himself. As far as getting away went, there'd be his car—Cockayne's car, that is, which he'd driven there earlier in the day, left somewhere accessible, ready for getting away."

"Cockayne wasn't likely to have missed it," Kite agreed; "he wasn't using it because of it failing its M.O.T." He stood up and walked to the window, turned his back on the Town Hall and sat on the sill.

"So we got the wrong corpse. We assume Fleming killed Cockayne. The only thing we don't know is which of them murdered Mitch."

"I think we'll have to assume that was Fleming too, though almost certainly it would've needed two of them to get him into the river. As I see it, that's why Cockayne kept quiet for a bit. Then he began to get windy and either threatened to confess or tried a bit of blackmail on Fleming. Either way, it became necessary for Fleming to get rid of him. So he got this idea of killing Cockayne, changing places with him and letting everyone believe him dead . . . and, you know, it wasn't impossible he might have got away with it, with both murders."

If questions about Mitch's death had led to the Gaiety, a possibility he couldn't afford to overlook, with himself, Fleming, supposedly dead and Cockayne supposedly having disappeared, suspicion of both murders would have rested on the absent Cockayne—as indeed it had. Faking his own death had therefore been necessary to allow him to disappear.

It had clearly not been a spur-of-the-moment killing. Risks had been taken to obtain the gun from Culver's house, and he'd been prepared with sleeping pills very likely taken from Georgina's supply. Fleming had even been prepared to sacrifice his car in the interests of verisimilitude—though that had been registered in Georgina's name and would in due course be returned to her. Which bore thinking about.

He had obviously intended to get right away and make a fresh start under another name. This would pose few problems to a man like Fleming, who was used to living a double life, on the edge of deception. Curious, then, about the money, his last-minute desperation for cash. Wouldn't he have taken care to have had ready the wherewithal necessary for his getaway, at least before he'd committed the murder? Because this time, in his new life, he wouldn't have had any handouts from Georgina to sweeten the pill. Unless Cockayne's threats had become so insistent that his immediate despatch became necessary, and unless . . .

It was impossible now to believe Georgina Fleming wasn't involved.

"She swears the last time she saw Fleming was on Sunday. I think

MORE DEATHS THAN ONE 137

she was lying. So what the hell," Mayo said grimly, "did she think she was playing at, leading us up the garden path, identifying the body as Fleming's?"

Lili Anand had always believed Ashleigh Cockayne was dead, so she took the news that they had found him stoically, her sorrow tempered by the fact that her predictions had been proved substantially correct, if somewhat confused regarding their application.

Would you have said they were alike, Lili? Fleming and Ashleigh Cockayne?" Mayo asked.

"No!" Her answer was vehement. Then, "Well, maybe they were physically alike, in a way. From behind, yes, you might just have mistaken them. They both had dark brown hair, they were similar in build. Slim and loose-limbed, you know. But Fleming was taller than Ashleigh, and they weren't in the least bit alike to look at." She paused. "So it was Fleming who killed Ashleigh? And that poor policeman too?" She nodded to herself, not needing an answer. "It's possible to believe. So where is he? If he isn't dead, where is Rupert Fleming?"

FIFTEEN

" 'Twill hardly buy a capcase for one's conscience."

A TELEPHONE CALL to Georgina Fleming's company the previous day had established that she was away on business for the day in Nottingham, would be staying overnight and travelling straight back to the office the following morning. Accordingly arrangements had been made to take up the first appointment of the following day at the office, where, the next morning, they made their way.

Centre Court was what the agents, when trying to lease it, had called a "prestigious office and shop development." Just off the new shopping precinct at the top of the town, it was a two-storey brick-built complex that tried hard not to offend by too-obvious functionalism, the buildings being of varying height and styles, some with bow windows and gables and steeply pitched roofs, all centred around a cobbled, glassed-in courtyard with a fountain surrounded by a planting of shrubs, entered through a pedestrian archway. Georgina Fleming's offices were on the ground floor of one of the blocks, next to a small café with a swinging sign.

Mayo paused to study the discreet nameplate by the door as they went through. "Culver Dixon Associates."

"*Culver.* Interesting, hm?"

"A lot of women nowadays prefer to keep their maiden name."

"Even when they've disassociated themselves with their father?"

Inside, the offices were carpeted throughout in caramel wall-to-wall, and decorated in toning shades of honey and cream. Heavy blue silk and champagne net hung at the windows, and there were plenty of pictures about, with lush displays of flourishing plants in the corners. Very stylish. Very expensive. A well-heeled look which made sense for a business consultancy, when you realized that the message was: 'This could happen to you too.'

Although they had arrived on the dot for their appointment, she kept them waiting on the blond leather seating in the reception area for a nicely calculated seven minutes. During that time, various women in various modes of dress from mini-skirts to trousers, passed through. A large lady arriving like a bat via the front entrance, wrapped in a flapping cloak, hair all over the place, hung about with Tesco carrier bags and clutching a briefcase under her arm gave them a quick appraisal and a professional smile *en passant,* as she made straight for the reception desk.

"Anything for me, Lisa?" she queried.

"Everything's on your desk, Mrs. Dixon."

A quick nod and she'd sailed past: Alison Dixon, presumably, Georgina's partner, possibly several years older than Georgina. There could hardly have been a greater contrast between the two women when, a couple of minutes later, Georgina herself appeared and led them back along the corridor into her office. She was wearing an olive-green suit with a burgundy silk shirt, shoes and tights to match, a great deal of gold costume jewellery. She looked terrific, despite the unapproachable manner, her obvious impatience. Waving them to chairs, she sat down herself and immediately began fiddling with a silver pencil. Tap-tap-tap. Impatient, Mrs. Fleming, impatient or nervous, or possibly both. The tension in the taut line of her jaw almost made Mayo's own jaw ache.

No sooner were they seated than a tray of coffee and biscuits arrived, obviously a standard procedure with visitors, brought in by an efficient-looking girl with large spectacles and a no-nonsense manner. Georgina Fleming poured. The coffee was very good, the biscuits in Kite's opinion nothing to speak of.

"There's been a development in the case which we think you should know about, Mrs. Fleming," he began, stirring his coffee.

"Oh?"

Mayo watched her closely while his sergeant, quickly swallowing the last of his biscuit, told her that the body she had identified was not that of her husband.

No astonishment showed on her face, no relief, no joy, but the silver pencil stopped its tapping. "Then who is it?" she asked, her voice quite steady.

"It's the body of a man called Ashleigh Cockayne."

"And who is Ashleigh Cockayne?"

"I should have thought you'd have known that, Mrs. Fleming," Mayo said. "Seeing he was a friend of your husband's. Arts Director for the Lavenstock Community Centre, where Mr. Fleming apparently spent a good deal of time."

"Oh, *that* Cockayne!" As though Ashleigh Cockayne was a name as common as Tom Smith or Jack Jones, as though the finding of his dead body might be regarded as an everyday occurrence too. "He may have mentioned him."

Mayo waited. She picked up the pencil again. Tap, tappy, tap-tap. Tap tap. "Mrs. Fleming," he said quietly, "I wonder if you've properly appreciated what we've been saying. Your husband is not dead. Forgive me if I'm mistaken, but I would've thought you'd have been surprised and happy at the news."

For the first time she let anger show in her face. Mayo was relieved to see it, to see that she was human after all, with "senses, affections, passions" . . . that if pricked, she could bleed. "Of course I'm surprised, of course I'm happy! What do you think I am? Did you expect me to faint, or jump up and down and clap my hands?"

Mayo thought a normal wife might have done either of these things, but not Georgina Fleming. "Do you know where your husband is?" he asked with an abrupt change of direction.

She was too astute to be caught out with a trick as old as that. "How should I? I thought he was dead, until five minutes ago."

"Yes of course, you identified him, didn't you?"

"I must have been mistaken."

"How d'you think you came to make such a serious mistake?"

"What are you suggesting? I didn't see his face, remember?"

"But you saw his body, his hands. A wife can usually recognise her husband's body, Mrs. Fleming. And his hands. Especially if he doesn't smoke, and the hands she's looking at are heavily nicotine-stained."

"I—I didn't notice that. I was very upset."

"You were very shocked. That's not quite the same thing."

She said nothing, her amber eyes and her poppy-lipsticked mouth were steady. He was impressed by the speed with which she'd regained her control, but he wondered just what was going on behind it. It was unnatural, you couldn't keep up that amount of self-restraint without paying a price, and it showed in the strain around her eyes. He suspected she was uncommunicative because she was afraid of what she might reveal of herself if she allowed herself to be otherwise, but her attitude wasn't something that was conducive to forwarding his enquiries, or indeed to helping herself. If she'd stopped to consider the absurdity of her attitude, she might have seen that she wasn't doing herself one little bit of good.

"It would help, Mrs. Fleming," he said with some asperity, "if you could try to be a little more forthcoming."

"I'm answering your questions. I don't know what more you want, I'm sure."

"Something called cooperation. I don't think I need remind you that a murder enquiry is hardly a trivial matter. And something else: your father's gun, to which you could have had access, was found near the body. The victim had been dosed with sleeping pills, and you have those in your possession. Do you understand what I'm saying?"

"I really hope not. But if you're saying I murdered this Ashleigh Cockayne, you're mad. I'd never even met the man."

"If we still thought the victim was your husband, I might well be saying you could have murdered *him*. As it is, I think it's more than possible you helped your husband to kill Cockayne. You identified Cockayne's body as Rupert Fleming's because if he was officially dead he couldn't be charged with Cockayne's murder."

"That's insane! I was mistaken, that's all, I was upset, anybody might have made the same mistake. And Rupert wouldn't murder anybody, any more than I would!"

"What would you say if I told you another body has been found?"

He felt, rather than heard, her quick intake of breath at that. He saw her stop herself from speaking, but only just. What had she been going to say? In the ensuing silence the air conditioner switched itself on with a hum, someone walked past with heavy footsteps in the corridor. "Another body you think I should know something about?" she said at last.

"I couldn't say that, Mrs. Fleming. Perhaps you can tell me if you do." He decided to tell her who the second body was and she looked shaken, but there was no mistaking also the relief. "Why should you think that should concern either me or Rupert?"

This was something he preferred to keep to himself for the moment, if she didn't really know, which he doubted, as he was beginning to doubt everything she said, so he skipped the answer. "If, as you believe, your husband has nothing to do with Ashleigh Cockayne's death, why has he gone missing? Where is he, Mrs. Fleming?"

"I've told you I don't *know*," she said flatly. "He'll be back as usual when it suits him, I've no doubt." The skin was tight over the bones of her face. She sat upright on her chair, without leaning back. The little silver pencil lay on the desk, unheeded. Mayo sighed.

"I'm going to give you the opportunity to reconsider the statement you made to us, in particular about the last time you saw your husband."

"I don't see why that should be necessary. I told you the truth, there's no need for me to alter anything I said."

"You stated," he reminded her, "that you last saw him on Sunday evening. Did you part on good terms?"

"Yes."

"Are you sure you didn't see him after that?"

"I'm certain."

"You didn't see him at any time on Monday?"

"No."

"All right, Mrs. Fleming, I'm going to leave it for now." He stood up and hooked his coat off the chair arm and Kite closed and pocketed his notebook, and then Mayo said, "How did your husband get on with his family?"

"His *family?*" She looked perfectly blank for an instant, then smiled faintly. "If Rupert got on with anyone in this world, it was with his mother."

"Thank you. Grateful for your time, Mrs. Fleming," he said ironically. "Good morning to you." At the door he turned and remarked in a conversational tone, "We'll find him, you know, with or without your help. I don't give up easily. But I think you'd do well to reflect on one or two things—one of which is that you are already in deep trouble yourself. It's a serious offence, deliberately misleading the police during the investigation of a murder. Think about it, Mrs. Fleming."

Marigold Vanstone drove soberly and carefully through the country lanes to the railway station, where she deposited her husband James and his briefcase to take his first-class seat on the London commuter train, accepted his perfunctory kiss and agreed that she would meet him off the seven-ten as usual. As she drove away towards Lavenstock, she picked up speed and began to sing.

The weather was perfect, bright and sunny, not a cloud in the sky. In the lanes catkins trembled on the alders, celandines gleamed in the hedgerows, blackbirds sang their mating call on the budding branches of the hawthorn and in the town centre the flower seller near the Town Hall had bunches of mimosa for sale. A stiff, chilly breeze was funnelling itself into a wind tunnel between the streets, but Marigold was well prepared with fur-lined boots, two thick sweaters, a padded coat and woolly mittens. She hadn't forgotten her long johns, either. It was cold work, standing all day at a market stall.

She did some necessary shopping and then drove on to the flea market. She always made a point of being one of the first to arrive, so as to get one of the better stalls. They were allocated in order of arrival, and she liked to have one near the Sheep Street entrance, and then her display was one of the first to catch people's eye as they came into the market.

Chuck Bradley was already there, setting up his wonderful collection of old ironmongery on the stall next to hers. This mostly comprised a conglomeration of ancient tools and electrical gear whose function defied definition, together with rusty scissors, shears, screwdrivers, old yellow-handled knives and bent-pronged forks. A jumble of unidentified metal parts was contained in various boxes, which he had labelled "Sundrys" in black felt-tip.

"Wotcher, Marigold."

" 'Morning, Chuck."

He was a huge, cheerful, treble-chinned man, dressed in a jacket that appeared to have been fashioned from a couple of horse blankets, and a fur hat with ear flaps. They'd become great pals since she'd first taken a stall here six or seven months ago.

"Look what I got here, darling." Gleefully Chuck brought out from his station wagon a battery radio in a solid-oak case, circa 1930, and put it in pride of place next to a Singer hand-operated sewing machine without a handle and a push-along mower with a broken blade. Marigold always wondered who would ever buy any of these defunct objects, but someone usually did.

Spreading the dark blue chenille tablecloth over her stall, she began to unload her own things onto it. Pretty bits of china, ornaments and bric-a-brac, most of them inexpensive, with a few genuinely old things in and among. It was a waste of time trying to sell anything with a high price tag. People came here looking for something for nothing, though the days when you could pick up genuine antiques for a song had long since disappeared. But it never failed to surprise her how much profit one could actually accumulate from the sale of such modest items.

She kept most of her good things at the shop. The thought of her own little business brought a smile to her lips. It still gave her a thrill of pride to read over the door "Marigold Antiques," never mind how James patronised it. It was a dear little shop of brick and timber construction, with low ceiling beams and many nooks and crannies inside, just right for displaying old furniture and china. It was a pity it was a little out of the way, for that meant she didn't get much in the way of passing trade. But she fully intended to alter all that. Taking the weekly stall here was part of her long-term strategy to add a little more to her capital, thus enabling her gradually to make enough money to buy some really good pieces, so that she'd become better known and then customers would make the special effort to seek her out. Of course, she didn't need the income, not with the privileged lifestyle accorded to the wife of a successful stockbroker, but she did need both the occupation, now that the children were grown up, and the confidence that doing something off her own bat gave her. She was determined to prove she could do it, if only to confound James's predictions.

Trade was unusually brisk that morning. The weather had brought shoppers out in cheerful mood and nobody made disparaging comments about Marigold's wares, or tried to haggle down the price. An old lady brought along some Goss souvenir jugs with "A Present from Swansea" printed on, which she wanted to sell and which Marigold was willing to buy. By midday she'd sold one of them, along with two underglaze blue and white plates, both slightly chipped, a beaded bag and a jet necklace to a personal friend who happened by, three ornate Edwardian hatpins, a cut-glass salt cellar and a couple of hall-marked silver teaspoons for twenty pounds each. Flushed with success, she said yes, she'd watch over Chuck's stall while he went to get them both a mug of tea from the snacks cabin in the corner.

And then occurred the sort of thing she'd always dreamed would happen but had never actually believed would. A fat, spotty youth in jeans and leather jacket stopped by her stall and casually pulled from one pocket a small teapot, elaborately painted and gilded, from the other its lid and stand. Coalport Imari, early nineteenth century. Genuine, she was sure, by the racing of her heart.

"You interested in buying this, then?" the youth asked offhandedly.

Marigold didn't show her excitement. She knew that would be fatal. She also knew immediately that he couldn't have come by the teapot honestly and that she must refuse to buy it from him. "Where did you get this?" she asked, examining it for flaws and finding none.

"It was me gran's."

She was sorely tempted, despite the lie. She happened to know just the person who would immediately pay almost anything she asked for old Coalport. And that she really ought *not* to touch it if it was even remotely suspect. She'd be a fool if she did. "I'll give you thirty pounds for it," she said in a rush, almost hoping he'd laugh in her face at such a derisory amount. But he goggled and then his expression turned sly and she knew she'd said too much and nearly given the game away. If she'd offered him ten pounds, he'd have taken it and thought himself lucky.

"Forty," he said.

She gulped. "Thirty-five."

He hesitated, but only for a moment. "Done."

She counted out seven five-pound notes and, as soon as he turned away to mingle with the crowd, put the teapot under the stall. Her hands were trembling so much she was afraid she might drop it.

"Here, what did *he* want?" Chuck asked, looming up with a pint mug of orange-coloured tea in each hand, nodding towards the disappearing youth.

"D'you know him?" She clutched the huge thick mug he gave her convulsively, warming her icy cold hands round it, grateful for the warmth, drinking greedily, though she'd forgotten to remind him about no sugar and he'd made it almost like syrup.

"Know him? Well, I know his old man better, but I wouldn't trust either of them as far as I could throw 'em—which wouldn't be a long way. What's he up to, then, been trying to sell you summink what dropped off the back of a lorry?"

"Oh, Chuck, how did you know?" She took another long drink of the over-sweet tea. "I think," she said mournfully, "I've just made a fool of myself. I can't *imagine* what came over me."

"Oh dear oh dear! Made a dishonest woman of you, has he?" Chuck roared with laughter, but then a customer claimed his attention and Marigold was left to her own thoughts, which consisted mainly of imagining herself in the Magistrates Court, or behind bars, with James disapprovingly saying, "I told you so." By the time Chuck had sold a couple of Vera Lynn 78s to his customer she could hardly wait to pour out the story.

"Well, don't get yourself into a tizz-woz, Marigold darling. Best thing you can do is take it down the nick. Ask for Mr. Mayo, D.C.I. Mayo, and tell him I sent you. He won't bite your head off, buys clock parts off of me sometimes. Mind you, I shouldn't tell him it like you've told me, darling, no need to say you knew it was hot before you bought it. Say it come to you afterwards, like," he finished with a grotesque wink.

"The police," Marigold said hollowly. The day no longer seemed quite so bright.

In the end, it wasn't Mayo she saw, but Atkins, whom nothing surprised anymore since he'd seen it all before. He took her story with a pinch of salt but didn't tell her so. He let her think he accepted what she said, that she'd only examined the teapot closely after the youth had gone, realized its value and that the youth's assertion of it belonging to his gran was unlikely to be true. He knew it was a piece of luck, which he looked forward to relaying to Mayo, especially since Mrs. Vanstone was able to give him the lad's name on account of the neighbouring stallholder, Chuck Bradley, a name well known to Atkins, having recognised him. Atkins was also acquainted with Sampson *père et fils*—Joey Sampson and his son Wayne, who ran a breaker's yard out on the by-pass. Any more he didn't need to know.

And since she'd acted no differently from the way a lot more people would have done, except that she was being more than usually honest in wanting to make retribution, and he thought it unlikely she'd do such a thing again, he thanked the lady for her cooperation, kept the teapot and said he'd follow the matter up. Marigold Vanstone went away looking hugely relieved that her departure from the straight and narrow had cost her no more than thirty-five pounds down the Swanee, as Chuck might say.

One little old teapot, Coalport Imari or whatever, looked very much like another to Atkins, but having compared this one with the coloured photographs of her property supplied by Lois French, there didn't seem much room for doubt.

"Farrar!" he called out. "Got a job for you, son. You're going to love this one, right up your street, it is."

SIXTEEN

"Can you weep Fate from its determined purpose?"

IT WAS JUST UNDER SEVEN MILES from the centre of Lavenstock to where the road turned into Scotley Beeches, just by the entrance to Fiveoaks Farm. Kite clocked it up and spoke the figure aloud to Mayo, sitting beside him as they drove past on the way to Derbyshire and the village where the elder Flemings now lived in their retirement. Mayo, preferring Kite to drive not only because he enjoyed taking the wheel, but because he was an abominable passenger, observed the place with interest and told him to pull in.

"Stop a minute and let's have a look at that coppice. It should be just round this next corner."

The place where Mayo had felt so sure that Fleming had left Cockayne's car was just beyond a sharp bend in the road. It comprised, they discovered, mainly sapling beech, ash and holly, growing in an undisciplined way that afforded quite dense cover, even this early in the season. They poked about for a while, but found nothing, as Farrar and Deeley had reported. Apart from the entrance to it, where many cars had evidently driven in either for a convenient pull-up off the road or else to venture further in where the cover was deeper, for reasons other than convenience, it seemed fairly undisturbed. The Volkswagen, especially at this time of year, might well have been left there for several days without anyone's noticing it. And no one *had* noticed it, or come forward to say they had, despite the appeal that had been put out.

"Only as I expected," Mayo grunted, settling back into the car. Leaning forward, he pressed the radio button, closed his eyes and forebore to say anything more. And for the first half of the journey, Kite was obliged to listen to Radio Three playing music by obscure Scandinavian composers and to something melancholy by Elgar for the rest. Mayo was quite silent, apparently asleep, but almost certainly not. How could he enjoy this stuff? Kite, hoping in vain that they'd play something from *The Phantom of the Opera*, or even a bit of his mother-in-law's favourite Gilbert and Sullivan, sighed and sped on.

There was a notable thinning of traffic now, when they reached the long, rolling roads over the Derbyshire moors. Fewer cars, fewer houses and people. Aware of the empty landscape rolling past, Kite felt as though he might as well be on the moon. The season was later up here. There had been a little snow along the tops, lightly powdering the moors, matching them to the limestone walls and giving the wide landscape an overall greyness, like a shroud. When they were within a couple of miles of their destination, Mayo sat up, switched the radio off and looked round to see where they were.

"Is it going to be worth the trouble, coming all this way to see the old folks?" Kite asked, feeling he could now speak. "Do you think Georgina Fleming's sent us off on a wild goose chase?"

"Wouldn't put it past her, but we shan't know that till we've spoken to them, shall we?"

"It's bound to be a shock. First hearing that your son's dead, then that he's not."

"That's partly why I decided to break the news in person," Mayo said. "It's not something you can convey on the telephone."

Partly it was that, and partly because he needed to watch their reactions when they were told, that he'd decided to make the journey. As Kite said, it was going to be a shock to the elder Flemings, who could scarcely have come to terms with the fact of his death yet, to hear their son was alive and Mayo felt an almost physical aversion to what lay ahead, but he couldn't afford finer feelings. If Fleming *had* been in touch with his parents since his apparent death, Mayo felt he would know and might then be able to get a line on Fleming's present whereabouts. He didn't think they would be able to conceal their knowledge that their son was alive. The Georgina Flemings of this world were few and far between, thank God.

The Old Manse turned out to be a square, grey stone house on the edge of a singularly charmless limestone-works village on one of the hills which surrounded Buxton, but its back was to the village and its large sash windows gave out over a magnificent view of the moors. The front garden rose steeply from the road in a series of terraces, along which small early rock plants were braving the bracing air. A small cold drizzle had begun and Kite shivered, turning up his collar and digging his hands into his pockets as they mounted the steps, Mayo likewise, realizing his blood, too, must have thinned since his days in the north.

The door was opened by an elegant, white-haired woman, rather bent but still slim, with a vague, sweet smile and lustrous dark eyes. She wore cashmere and soft tweed, and her hands on the handle of a silver-knobbed stick were heavily ringed with big old jewels that slid about on her thin fingers.

"You're the police," she greeted them in a pleasant contralto. "Please come in."

Drifting before them, using the stick more like an Edwardian parasol than an aid to walking, she led the way into the drawing room at the front of the house, a cold room with a high ceiling and white walls, which the fully turned on gas fire did little to heat. It was furnished with heavy handsome antiques and Georgian chairs with slippery upholstery, fine old silver in a corner cabinet, Chinese porcelain on the mantelpiece. A room looking and smelling as if it were polished every Friday and never used.

"Excuse me," Mrs. Fleming said, "I'll get my husband, he's in the other room. Oh, here he is. Guy, they're here."

Guy Fleming was a tall stork-like figure buttoned into a cardigan, still a good-looking man, though by now in his late seventies, with the sort of lofty profile the Victorians used to call "noble." His expression was benign, his smile and his handshake warm and ready, and Mayo wondered why he felt there was something empty and insubstantial about him, as if he were not really flesh and blood but a cut-out fashioned from cardboard. He had been something high and mighty in his company, but it was hard to imagine that now. Perhaps he was one of those men who need an image of themselves to believe in, and without the corporate identity there was nothing left to live up to.

They made a fine pair, and it was easy to see where Rupert Fleming had got his good looks. Mayo needn't have worried about breaking news which, however he put it, was bound to be painful.

Though elderly, the couple were all there, and he was relieved that at least the meeting would be conducted on a basis of mutual intelligence, though Mrs. Fleming was beginning to unnerve him slightly with the unexpected perception of her gaze.

"They don't want that muck," the old man growled when she announced that if they wanted coffee she would get the girl to bring it in, "get them a proper drink!"

But Mayo declined both suggestions with thanks. They hadn't made such good progress as he'd hoped from Lavenstock and, judging by the savoury smell issuing from the back quarters, lunch was evidently in the offing. In any case, he was impatient to get on.

"I'm sorry to have to intrude on your grief," he began, "but perhaps you'll understand when you've heard what I have to say."

Mrs. Fleming looked down at her folded hands, then raised her eyes. "Please go on."

He was watching them both and it was the old man's eyes that filled with tears when he began to speak of their son. It was hard to tell what Mrs. Fleming was thinking, with that dark, deep, slightly ironic regard fixed on him. Hard to go on, too. How did you say, "The good news is that your son has not been killed, the bad news is that he is a murderer"? There was no easy way, in fact, for them to hear what he had to say, even though he omitted as much detail as he could and left out any mention of Mitch's death. When he'd finished, there was a long silence. The old man looked stunned. "Did you hear that, Muriel?" he asked at last. "Rupert's still alive!"

Mrs. Fleming's remarkable eyes remained fixed on Mayo. "Are you sure of that?"

"We've no reason to think otherwise."

"Why were you so certain it was Rupert who was dead in the first place?" The questions were decisive and he saw that her vagueness was an illusion which she chose to foster and use when she felt it was expedient.

"He was in your son's car, wearing his watch. Rupert's jacket was there, with his wallet and papers in it. A suicide note was left in his handwriting. And his wife identified him as her husband."

She nodded briefly but at the mention of Georgina her lips compressed and he saw there was no love lost there.

"He's not dead!" the old man repeated in wonder. He appeared not to have heard what else had been said. "Oliver, we must tell Oliver. His brother, you know," he explained to Mayo.

"Guy!" Mrs. Fleming turned slowly towards him, speaking to him with compassion, enunciating slowly as if he were a child or a person of limited intelligence. "Don't you understand what they're saying, my dear? They think Rupert is the one who—who took this other man's life." Despite her calm reception of the news, her deep voice shook a little, either with emotion or with one of the involuntary tremors of old age. Her hands were convulsively clenched on the arms of her chair, the jewels flashing fire where the light caught them. "That is what you think, isn't it?" she asked Mayo.

"I'm afraid it's a strong possibility."

She nodded several times and then suddenly, startling him, smiled, a very beautiful, transforming smile. "But, you know, that's absolute rubbish."

It wasn't an unexpected response. She would protect her son with every fibre of her being, fight for him like a tigress because she simply would never admit that any son of hers was capable of committing murder. It was the same blind spot, the same unshakeable belief in their child's innocence he'd seen in countless other mothers, the same serene certainty. Unfortunately, such faith in their errant lambs hardly ever turned out to be justified.

Rupert's father did not appear to share her convictions, either. "So it's come to that, has it by God?" he quavered. "To *murder!*"

"Never," said the mother. "That's quite absurd. There must be some mistake."

"Muriel, he's never given us anything but trouble. And now, this. Oliver now, he's been everything a son should be, but Rupert . . ." He faltered for a moment. "And yet, you know, I always loved him best."

"Guy Fleming, I'm surprised at you. Your own son! There was nothing wrong with Rupert, until he married that woman, nothing that wouldn't have righted itself, given time. Pull yourself together, Guy."

The effect of these bracing words on him was immediate, though not perhaps in the way she would have wished. He seemed to be literally obeying her orders, pulling his shoulders back and sitting more stiffly upright. He said stubbornly, "Nothing could ever have put Rupert right. No, I shall speak, Muriel. The whole thing is too much for me at my age. He was always an unsatisfactory child, and nothing's changed. Expelled from school, failing his accountancy exams, losing the insurance position . . ."

It was then that Mrs. Fleming began to show her mettle. "That's enough," she ordered. "Quite enough. The Chief Inspector doesn't want to hear your prattle."

She was wholly wrong. It was exactly what Mayo did want to hear. But it was too late. As if the effort had been too great, Fleming passed a hand across his face and subsided, and before Mayo could frame further questions, the door opened and a young woman stood there. Hesitating on the threshold, she waited until Muriel Fleming beckoned before crossing the room to sit beside her on the sofa. "I don't believe a word of it either," she said as they exchanged looks, entirely in accord.

This, presumably, was "the girl" Mrs. Fleming had mentioned, who would have brought the coffee in, had they wished it. She still looked sad and solemn, but she'd discarded her dreary, penitential black for similar garments in shades of green, brown and ochre that looked as if they had been hand-dyed with vegetable colouring, and probably had. There was no mistaking her. It was Bryony Harper.

Mrs. Fleming was watching Mayo with a detached, ironic amusement while he recovered his momentarily scattered forces. Having the advantage, and with perfect composure, she beat him to it with a return of her vague smile and a slightly rambling explanation of Bryony's presence.

"This dear girl, whom I believe you've met," she began, "wrote to us to offer her sympathy as soon as she heard about Rupert. Can you imagine anything kinder or more thoughtful? In her position? We'd never heard of her before, but we knew Rupert's marriage wasn't all it should be, so we weren't entirely surprised that he should have found someone else. Bryony mentioned her children and we thought"—a fleeting look of disappointment crossed her face—"well, never mind, we took the car down to Lavenstock and brought her and the little boys back here with us. She'd made our son happy, it was the least we could do. And here she's going to stay, aren't you, my dear?"

The permutations of human beings and their behaviour patterns had long since ceased to be a source of amazement to Mayo, but this unexpected turn of events gave him a moment's pause, and an exchange of glances showed that Kite was equally taken aback.

"If I may," Bryony was saying. "For a while, at least." She explained to Mayo, "The boys are happy here. They love being spoiled and having other children next door to play with." The two women looked at each other again, a certain complicity in their smiles. Their eyes were very alike, deep and dark, but whereas Bryony's were wide, naive and trusting, Mrs. Fleming's were observant and not easily fathomable.

Mayo cleared his throat and asked Bryony how much she'd overheard of what he'd been telling Mr. and Mrs. Fleming, hoping he wouldn't have to go over everything again.

"I heard you saying that it wasn't Rupert who was dead—and that you think he might have killed this other man, but"—and there was a world of misery in her face—"that can't possibly be true." Her voice broke, tears weren't far away.

"I'm afraid we can't fly in the face of facts."

"There must be some other explanation," she whispered, shaking her head and adding with some inner logic that was not apparent to anyone else, "I *know* he's innocent."

"If he is, then why has he disappeared?"

"Because he's in deep trouble . . . oh, I know he must be involved somehow, and that's really bad, but it's crazy to imagine he'd kill someone and try to pass himself off as dead!"

He looked at her steadily and after a while her eyes dropped. He said sternly, with a growing conviction that he was on the right lines, "Isn't there something you ought to be telling me?"

"No! Yes, I—don't know . . ." She looked frightened and turned her head, refusing to meet his gaze.

Mrs. Fleming uttered a quiet "Bryony!" while her husband, bewildered, looked from one to the other.

The girl sat twisting her hands together. "I'm sorry," she said in a low voice to Mrs. Fleming. "I must. If I tell them, it may help them to find him."

"I can't stop you," Mrs. Fleming said, "but I hope you won't be sorry."

To Mayo, Bryony said, "I've had a letter from him, you see. He wouldn't have sent it if he wanted everyone to believe he was dead, would he?"

The old man, giving an odd little grunt of shock, sank back into his chair with an air of defeat and closed his eyes, absolving himself from further involvement.

Mayo said woodenly, "I think you'd better tell me about this."

"It came the day after you came to see me. It wasn't exactly a letter, just a note. He said he had to go away for a while, and he enclosed some money for me and the children. He obviously knew you were going to suspect him and that's why he made the decision to go away. I don't think that was very sensible, but it's understandable, isn't it? And . . . and in the middle of all that he still managed to be concerned about me and took the trouble to send me all that money. That's not the sort of thing he'd do if he was the kind who'd do the things you're suggesting."

There was no sort of logic in this, but logic has never played a great part where love is concerned, and of that Bryony Harper had no lack. He asked, as tactfully as he could, how much money there had been with the letter.

"An awful lot. About a thousand pounds, as a matter of fact."

"Money doesn't go very far these days, Bryony. A thousand pounds isn't all that much."

"It is to me," she said simply.

Mayo felt the same mixture of exasperation and pity he'd felt at their previous meeting. Her complete trust in Fleming was amazing to him, especially since he was as convinced as he had ever been in his life that there was no basis whatever for it, that it was completely unjustified.

"Did you keep the letter?" he asked, without much hope. People hardly ever did, but there was just a chance that Bryony, with her incurably sentimental outlook on life, might have done so. He wasn't surprised when she said she'd thrown it away, but not sure whether she was telling the truth. It might have been that she simply didn't want to part with it.

"Do you still have the money?"

"Apart from a hundred pounds or so. I had bills and things to settle before I came here."

"I'm afraid I shall have to ask you for it, at least for the time being," he told her, explaining there would be tests to carry out on it. She looked dismayed, but Guy Fleming was heard to murmur unexpectedly from the depths of his chair that she need never be short of money while he was around and eventually she left the room to get it.

All this time Mrs. Fleming sat rigidly disapproving, her hands on the knob of the stick, saying nothing. There was, after all, little she could say. She roused herself to bid them a cool goodbye when they went, but it was left to Bryony to show them to the door.

As they drove away, he looked again at the envelope she had given him, addressed to her at the Morvah Pottery in Fleming's distinctive handwriting. It was postmarked Coventry, two days after his supposed death.

"So he's done it after all, he's got away, blast him. He must've already managed to sell the things he stole from Lois French," Kite said with some bitterness as they drove away, unaware that part of the goods in question was at that moment being steadily contemplated by George Atkins through a wreath of his evil pipe smoke as it stood in a place of honour in a specially cleared space on his desk.

"I suppose it's possible."

Otherwise, how had Fleming, who had apparently been casting around for any spare cash he could lay his hands on, been able to send Bryony Harper a thousand pounds in notes? Though perhaps he'd already had this money set aside, intending her to have it after his disappearance, and even though he'd been unable to drum up more, he'd sent it regardless. As a theory this was too unconvincing to appeal to Mayo. For one thing, why should Fleming destroy the myth of his own death he'd been at such pains to construct? For another, such selflessness and provident forethought seemed foreign to Fleming's nature as he'd come to see it.

And yet . . . what did he really know of Fleming? What kind of man was he, to live the uneasy, divided life he had lived? Basically a self-destructive life, willfully damaging to himself as well as to others, almost as though he had a death wish. Only Bryony seemed to have escaped the compulsion he seemed to have to destroy, to spoil, to wreck, perhaps because she was basically innocent, almost, one might be tempted to think, to the point of simpleness.

SEVENTEEN

"A wondrous necessary man, my lord."

THE LITTLE COALPORT TEAPOT, pretty enough if you liked that sort of thing, sat on Atkins's desk, giving little indication of its value. It was simply a small, frippery object, according to Kite hardly big enough to make a decent-sized cuppa. "Strewth!" he exclaimed on hearing its estimated value.

"Like a lot more things, size has nowt to do with it, lad," said Atkins. "It's quality that counts."

Mayo recognised it immediately. It had stood on a little round table that was covered with an antique silk shawl, not the most valuable of the things Fleming had appropriated, but to the uninitiated the flamboyance of its gold decoration might easily have made it seem so.

"Who's this yobbo you said was trying to flog it, George?" Kite was asking.

"Name of Sampson. Wayne Sampson. His dad has that car breaker's up the by-pass . . . and you know who that used to belong to, don't you?"

Kite cast his mind around until light broke. "Of course, I'd forgotten that."

"Sold it a good few years back, mind, but it'd be the first place he'd think of, wouldn't it, in the circumstances?"

"Is this a private discussion, George," Mayo said, clearing an airspace through Atkins's tobacco smoke with a waft of his hand, "or can anyone join in? Who's that you're talking about? And for God's sake, do us a favour and put those old socks out, will you?"

"I was forgetting. Before your time, that'd be." Atkins obligingly knocked out the noxious dottle of his pipe, thus creating an additional dimension to the odour already created, and explained:

"Sampson's yard used to be owned by John Culver till he sold it sometime back, maybe eight or nine years since."

"*Culver?*" All at once it began to seem possible that several unrelated elements might be part of the whole. "But the fact that Culver once owned the yard doesn't explain how this little thing, lifted by Fleming from Mrs. French's flat, could have got into the hands of someone like young Sampson."

Atkins said, "We should be about to find out. Farrar's already there."

D.C. Keith Farrar was indeed there, in this graveyard for the aspirations of the affluent society, picking his way fastidiously through the debris. His blond hair was neat and shining as ever, his shoes impeccably polished, his face clean-shaven and cheerful, his eyes alert. Nobody would have guessed that at least half-a-dozen worries skittered about beneath that debonair surface . . . whether his wife Sandra might be pregnant or not, the unforeseen rise in his mortgage, the non-event of his promotion, Sandra's fear that he might cop it one day, like Mitch, the very present danger that he might get oil on his good suit . . .

None of this showed, and presently he stopped and looked around but could see nothing that moved. The yard was unusually quiet, apart from the noise of a battered lorry, stacked with car bodies crushed flat like silver paper, idling in neutral. To one side, a crane reared its jib, the temporarily unemployed huge stone crusher suspended from it by four chains. Canyons created by the towering piles of rusting scrap bodies waiting for its attention led off in all directions. Farrar peered around a stack of used tyres and, backing away, skidded on a patch of thick black oil, nearly losing his balance. "The hell with this for a lark!" he muttered and stood where he was. "Anybody home?" he shouted. "Anybody home?"

An unsavoury figure with a spotty face, greasy hair and highly unsuitable winkle-picker boots with elaborate silver buckles and toecaps appeared reluctantly at the end of one of the canyons and watched him approach apprehensively. Wayne knew who Farrar was, having had him pointed out once by one of his mates as somebody to watch, and therefore having a good idea what he'd come for.

Didn't look much of a menace, poncey type like that, but you never knew with the fuzz. He decided he'd better not tell any more lies than he had to.

"Going into the antique business, I hear, young Sampson?" Farrar began when they were within talking distance.

"Dunno what you're on about," answered Wayne, predictably enough.

"Come on, lad, you were flogging a valuable bit of old china down the market this morning, and don't bother to deny it. Where'd you get it?"

"Found it."

"Thousands wouldn't believe you."

"It's bloody true!"

"I thought you said it belonged to your gran?"

"Well, I mean . . ." said Wayne.

"*What* d'you mean? You mean you nicked it?"

"No, I never! You got no right saying that."

"Come on then, where's the rest?"

"What rest? I don't know nothink about no rest."

Wayne scratched his spots, stuck his hands into the pockets of his dirty green overalls and lounged against the rusty body of a Ford Transit van, affecting nonchalance. Farrar looked at him with distaste. "I'm waiting."

"What for?"

Farrar said nothing, but a gleam appeared in his eye that Wayne thought best not to ignore. "S'right, whether you believe me or not," he protested indignantly. "Shoved out the way under the seat of a clapped-out old VW, it was, in an 'Arrods bag. Didn't think much to it, only a tatty old teapot, but I've seen things like that down the market, so I reckoned I might get a couple of nicker for it."

"That tatty old teapot was worth nearly a grand," Farrar said, exaggerating, though not very much, in the interests of getting this over with. "And it was only part of what was in that Harrods bag. If you can't produce the rest, and quick, you're in dead schtuck, sunshine."

Wayne went as green as his overalls, whether from chagrin at hav-

ing let the teapot go for a rotten thirty-five nicker or fear that he
might be wading in deeper waters than he'd thought, it wasn't possible to say, but that was all one to Farrar.

"Well," the youth said, after some painful wrestling with his natural reluctance to give anything away to the fuzz, "they might still be
in the office," jerking his head towards the corrugated-roofed edifice
in the corner.

"That's better. We'll have a shufty in a minute, but before we do
you can tell me about this Volkswagen and where it came from. Still
got it, have you?"

"You must be joking. Went under the crusher same day as it come
in," Wayne averred. A clapped-out old Beetle it'd been and no, he
neither knew nor bloody cared who'd brought it in or where it had
come from. The old man'd know, but he wasn't in just now. There
were no licence plates on it and the tax disc had been removed. He'd
seen it in the yard and given it the once-over as he always did before
letting any car go under the crusher. You'd never believe what you
found sometimes, what some daft nerks left in their cars. Things
worth more than the car. Radios, clocks, cigarettes, cassettes in the
glove box . . . they'd once found a case of malt whisky in the boot.

"Same way you just *found* that Coalport teapot and the other
stuff."

"I did, yeah, if that's what you call it, and if I hadn't, they'd have
gone the same way as the body! Why shouldn't I keep what I found
there? Nobody else was wanting the bloody things," Wayne protested, but tokenly, his vocabulary as limited as his intelligence. He
knew he hadn't a chance, and when Farrar questioned him about
what else had been in the car, he admitted there might've been a
holdall—with some gear in it, shirts and stuff, straight gear, he
sniffed, when pressed, evidently so far beneath his notice that he'd
left the bag where it was in the boot, along with a briefcase with
papers in it that held no interest for him.

"You've forgotten the typewriter."

"No I haven't, there wasn't no typewriter."

"Do me a favour! You've flogged that as well, haven't you, you
little toerag?"

Wayne had always been one to know when he was beaten. He

might have argued that appropriating the articles was one of the perks of his trade, but he gave in and admitted that he'd sold the typewriter at another market stall and that he still had the residue of what had been found in the plastic bag. Skirting the piles of car engines that lay about in black, shining, oily clusters, he led Farrar towards the shed in the corner that they called the office. They were almost there when a silver-coloured Mercedes bumped across the uneven dirt surface of the yard and out of it climbed the older, even fatter version of Wayne who was Sampson senior.

"Well, if it isn't Mr. Farrar!" Wayne's parent said, his eyes going from his unlovely son to the detective, quickly calculating which direction the trouble might spring from. "Can I help you?"

"Hello, Joey. Yes, I rather think you might. It's a little matter of a grey S Reg Volkswagen. Let's be having a dekko at your records. For your sake, I hope they're all nice and up-to-date."

"Who did you say?" Kite said incredulously into the phone. "You sure? All right, all right. Thanks anyway, Keith. Get yourself back here. That was Farrar," he relayed unnecessarily, putting the phone down. "He says it wasn't Culver who had the Beetle taken into the scrapyard."

"I don't think he's going to be too difficult," Mayo remarked, looking out of the small rear window in his office and watching Tim Salisbury cross the car park. "I know his type—all wind and puff."

He came into Mayo's office wearing a tweed cap pulled well down and a supercilious expression underneath it. He also had on a green padded sleeveless jacket over a thick sweater. It was very cold outside and rain threatened again.

"Good of you to come, Mr. Salisbury," Mayo began courteously, pretending an assumption that Salisbury had any option in the matter.

"I was coming into the bank, anyway," Salisbury said expansively, but with an equal pretence of not otherwise being prepared to put himself out. Mayo smiled, allowing him his illusions, and invited him to take a chair. A cup of tea was offered and with a barely repressed shudder almost refused, but then, with something like condescension, accepted. When the tea appeared Salisbury took one sip and left it alone. "What is it you want?"

"I won't beat about the bush. First, I'd like to know why you arranged for an S Registration Volkswagen to be towed into Sampson's breaker's yard on the fifteenth of March."

A lengthy pause ensued before Salisbury consented to answer. The thin veneer of his affability had already worn through. "Should've thought that was obvious. I reserve the right to dispose of derelict cars—or anything else for that matter—dumped on my land without my permission, without having to explain why. It's not an Irish tinker's scrapyard, you know."

"Who said the car was derelict?"

"Since it was practically falling to pieces, and nobody was claiming it, I assumed it was."

"Wasn't it rather high-handed of you to dispose of it without trying to find its owner? Why didn't you report it to us and let us sort it out?" Salisbury shrugged, deigning to reply. "And perhaps you'd care to tell me why you first removed the licence plates, and the tax disc?"

Salisbury's eyes flickered. "Who says I did that?"

"They weren't there when the car was towed into the scrapyard. Nor was the log book, for that matter." Pity he hadn't checked the boot too, but Mayo didn't feel it necessary to say so. "What happened to them?"

"I don't have to answer these questions."

"It would be in your own interests to do so."

"I think I may be the best judge of that."

"Do you? I don't believe you are, you know. Perfectly reasonable questions, Mr. Salisbury. But since you won't answer, you'll have to allow us to put our own construction on events. I suggest you had the vehicle towed away because you knew who'd left it there, first removing the identification because you'd very good reasons indeed for not wanting it to be known who it belonged to."

"I refuse to be badgered like this!"

"Nobody's badgering you, sir, and you're quite at liberty to refuse to answer, but the owner of that car has been murdered, and like it or not you're involved in the enquiries, if only as a result of your having his car towed away."

Salisbury had removed his cap on entering the room and now he undid the zip on his jacket. Perspiration stood on his forehead and his colour was high, his pale, prominent eyes bulging like marbles. He pulled out his handkerchief, wiped off the sweat. "Is that who it belonged to, that man Cockayne?"

"Are you telling me you didn't know that?"

A telephone rang insistently in the distance. No one answered it for some time. "I didn't *know,*" Salisbury admitted at last. "But I suppose I guessed it did."

"Does that mean you're prepared to make a statement?"

"I'm prepared to tell you what I know, if that's what you mean."

Mayo gave the go-ahead to Jenny Platt, whom he had asked to be present with her notebook, sitting in a corner by the window. She was an expert shorthand writer, far speedier and more accurate than Kite, who sometimes had trouble deciphering his own cryptic notations.

"Go on, Mr. Salisbury. Just tell me in your own words what happened."

Salisbury fidgeted for a while, gaining time, and then said, "Well, I was coming home that evening—"

"Which evening are we talking about?"

"The Monday evening, as I recall, the night before you came to the farm. I'd been to an N.F.U. meeting, as I told you then, which had gone on rather late, and I'd stayed on, talking to friends—"

"Just a minute. Let's be clear about the time."

"It was well after midnight, I suppose, I wouldn't like to swear to the exact time."

"All right, carry on."

"I was just coming out of the corner round by the lower coppice, going slowly because I was tired and the roads were icing over—you remember how frosty it was that night—when my headlights showed somebody moving about in the corner of the field, just behind the trees. I thought it was somebody poaching. We've had a lot of trouble lately, so I took my gun and got out to see. It was Fleming. Actually, I didn't recognise him at first, I hardly knew him and it must've been twelve months since I'd last seen him anyway, but he recognised me, immediately I think. He said, 'What the hell d'you think you're doing with that gun? Put it down for Christ's sake, it might go off.' " He paused to mop his forehead again.

"You look warm, Mr. Salisbury. Why not take your jacket off?"

He didn't appear to have heard, but put his handkerchief away and carried on. "I asked him what the hell *he* thought he was doing on my land, which was more to the point."

"And what did he say to that?"

"He laughed and said he'd be only too happy to get off it if he could get the damn car started and then he said, very offensively I thought, 'Why don't you see if you can help instead of just standing there?' I told him I was no mechanic, cleaning the plugs is about my limit, and actually it was such a pathetic old wreck it looked as though it'd never start again, anyway. So I suggested he leave it and come up to the house to ring for a taxi, which I thought was pretty generous in the circumstances, considering his tone."

"Did he accept?"

"He did not! He'd the blasted cheek to say he'd a better idea . . . why didn't I push off and leave him alone if that was the best I could do. He actually," Salisbury went on, his face becoming so suffused that his collar looked tight, "put his hand on my shoulder and shoved so that I staggered backwards."

"Then what happened?"

"Nothing happened, except that I did just that," Salisbury said shortly. "I pushed off and left him to it."

"Really? Are you quite sure that's all you did?"

Salisbury looked down his patrician nose. "You can please yourself whether you believe me or not, I've told you what happened," he said coldly.

Mayo considered him. "You just walked away. Now I wonder why?" He didn't think Salisbury in the least likely to take kindly to having his offer of help thrown back in his face. To shrug off the snub and simply walk away in circumstances like that was out of character.

"I'll tell you why," Salisbury said suddenly, leaning forward. "He looked bloody dangerous, that's why. It wasn't a suggestion he

made, it was a threat. If I'd refused, he was just as likely to have
knocked me down and made off with the Range Rover. I've a wife
and children, Mr. Mayo, I'd no right to start thinking of playing the
jolly old hero. And besides, strange as it may seem, I value my own
skin. I think even you might have thought twice about arguing with
him."

Mayo listened to this and felt that if this was the true reason, he
was inclined to like Salisbury better for it than at any time during
their short acquaintance. "So, what happened next?"

"What happened next was that Susan found him dead in his car
the following day, in case you've forgotten."

"No, I'm not likely to have forgotten that," Mayo answered
evenly. "I'm sorry for it, finding a body isn't a very pleasant experience, one I wouldn't wish on anyone, but it's somewhat beside the
point at the moment. Why didn't you mention what had happened
between you and Fleming when we spoke to you that night?"

"I panicked, like anybody else would. Wouldn't have looked very
good if I'd said we'd quarrelled just before he was murdered, would
it? While we were arguing, at least two cars passed and I was afraid
their headlights might've picked us out. I was holding my shotgun,
remember? And Fleming had pushed me so that I staggered."

Mayo considered him. "But you know by now that it wasn't Fleming who was murdered."

"Yes," Salisbury said shortly, "and I think myself lucky not to have
met the same fate, all things considered."

"All right, but when you first heard about Fleming's death, when
you thought he'd committed suicide in Scotley Beeches, apparently
shortly after you'd encountered him with the Volkswagen, you must
surely have thought that very odd. What did you think had happened?"

"My God, what a question! I didn't know what to think, except
that he must've gone back into the forest for some reason after I'd
spoken to him. There's a footpath that would've taken him there in
about fifteen minutes—and I assumed that's what he'd done."

"What did you think he'd been doing with the Volkswagen?"

"I don't know, I didn't *want* to know. All that bothered me was to
get it off my land, pronto, and that's what I told her . . ."

"Her?" Mayo said quickly.

There was a measurable silence. Jenny Platt's hand remained poised over her book. Salisbury suddenly picked up the despised, now cold tea and drank it off at one swig. "Georgina," he said. "Georgina Fleming."

Mayo sat back. "So, you and Mrs. Fleming were in this together."

"No, we were not!" Stung, Salisbury's voice had risen. "Not like that, not as you put it!"

"How would you put it, then?"

"I know nothing about this murder . . . at first, when I heard about Fleming—when you told us it was supposed to be Fleming who'd shot himself—I rang Georgina to offer my condolences." His prominent pale eyes were wary. "We used to know each other rather well some time ago, and though we hadn't seen each other for ages, I felt it was the least I could do."

"Very commendable, sir." And no doubt he had also wanted to know how the land lay, what line the police were taking and how much they knew and what his own course of action ought to be. "And I suppose you talked about the Volkswagen."

"Of course we did. I wasn't too happy, to put it mildly, at the idea of leaving it where it was under the circumstances."

"And Mrs. Fleming?"

"She knew nothing about it, until I told her. She was as mystified as I was as to why her husband was there messing about with that old banger when he had a perfectly good car of his own. And then, when he was found dead in the Porsche . . . well, whatever, I didn't want the VW leaving where it was, and Georgina saw my point. I told her I'd dispose of it and we both agreed it would be better all round to say nothing to anyone else about it. And I might say," he added bitterly, "I paid that scrapyard over the odds to do the same."

"Shouldn't be so trusting. And afterwards, when you learned it *wasn't* Rupert Fleming, but another man who'd been killed?"

"I realized then, of course, that he'd probably been trying to get away, but the car had been destroyed by then so there was no point in saying anything at that stage."

"Not even when we put out an appeal for information on the

Volkswagen?" Salisbury said nothing and Mayo's gaze on him was
hard. "I wonder if you're telling us the whole truth?"

Salisbury's face was stiff with dislike. "I'm not in the habit of
lying—" He broke off, looking discomfited, as if wondering whether
evasion came under the same heading and then deciding to brazen it
out. "Take it or leave it, I've told you what happened. If you don't
choose to believe me, that's your pigeon."

"I don't think you quite realize the situation you're in. What
you've been at pains to show as nothing more than a bit of an
argument with Fleming might well have been something much
worse. On your own admission, you had a gun with you. Fleming
was in a vicious mood that night, he may have just killed one man
and he'd nothing to lose by having a go at another. Are you quite
sure he didn't? Have a go? Or try to take your Range Rover, and did
you then perhaps use your gun? Is that perhaps why he hasn't been
seen since?"

Salisbury scraped back his chair and stood up. "I think you're
exceeding your authority, Chief Inspector," he said, hauteur in his
bulging blue eyes, gathering his forces but by no means as confident
as when he'd first come in.

Mayo could see what was coming and before Salisbury had the
chance to invoke friends in high places—the name of the Chief
Constable was hanging tangibly in the air—he stood up, too.
"Thank you for your time, Mr. Salisbury," he said. "We'll be in
touch. I shall want to see you again."

The two detectives sat for some time in silence after the door had
closed behind Jenny Platt, who had escorted Salisbury downstairs to
where his statement would be prepared for signature.

His departure left behind a sense of anti-climax. It wasn't within
the character of either man to want to admit that Fleming had got
away, but a realistic assessment of the situation had to allow that it
was possible he had—for the time being. To think of him permanently free, cocking a snook at them from somewhere out there, was
untenable to a degree. Finding him and bringing him to justice was a
top priority. A man who was capable of committing two murders of
such brutality had forfeited any right to freedom. Mayo was short on

sympathy for Fleming and others like him. He'd seen too much of the other side.

"We know the car *was* in the coppice at any rate," Kite said, "and we also know Fleming didn't get away in it as he'd planned. I suppose it's safe to assume he was in Coventry two days later, because of the letter being posted there."

"The old Volks could only have been a means of getting away in the first place. He must've had better arrangements in view for later."

"And if that was kaput, he'd either have to thumb a lift into Lavenstock, or maybe the opposite direction, or walk, before getting himself over to Coventry one way or another. Or even sleep in the car until next morning and then do likewise."

"Leaving behind, fortunately for us, his holdall, his typewriter, his briefcase and the things he'd been at so much trouble to steal from Lois French . . . it won't do, old lad, it won't do."

Kite thought for a moment. "He has to be somewhere around still."

Considering the situation, Mayo sat back, physically relaxed, but with an expression on his face with which Kite was familiar, that he knew boded no good for anyone on the wrong side of him. Stubborn, bloody-minded even, it also reflected his own inclinations at that moment.

"There is, however," Mayo said suddenly, "another alternative." And ten minutes of conversation later, he pushed the telephone across the desk to Kite.

It was half past three when Kite rang Culver Dixon Associates, and when he asked to speak to Mrs. Fleming he was told she had already left. It was her night at the squash club, but she'd asked her secretary to cancel the game she'd arranged to play, saying she had another appointment.

"Never mind, Martin." Mayo pushed back his chair with a sudden access of energy and shrugged himself into his jacket. "It won't matter in the long run, will it?"

EIGHTEEN

" 'Tis time to die when 'tis a shame to live."

"YOU WANTED TO SEE ME. Well, here I am, Father."

"Come in, girl, come in to the front."

In the cave of his study, Culver poked the fire to a blaze before lowering himself into his old wing chair while Minty, still wary of Georgina, turned around several times before curling on the hearth-rug at his feet. She was a one-man dog, Culver's and no one else's. She'd been brought to Upper Delph as a puppy seven years ago, a few weeks after Georgina had gone, never leaving his side since. She would take neither food nor orders from anyone other than him.

So little had anything changed in this room that Georgina felt she might have been back in her childhood, on this dark afternoon of flickering firelight—watching Andy Pandy on the television maybe, or later, when she was older, toasting crumpets at the fire with the long-handled brass fork, and her father puffing at his old pipe in the chair opposite. She was surrounded by objects well loved and famil-iar from her childhood . . . the wall clock, the Victorian watercolour she'd always loved of the house, and the old brown sofa that was a piece of her life. She remembered cuddling into the sofa's soft velvety comfort to read, or to watch her father draw pictures for her. Remembered too, hiding her face against the back and fighting to control tears she mustn't ever show.

"Don't ever let anybody know what you're thinking or feeling, girl. That way you'll always have the advantage." That's what he'd drummed into her, so that although they were never physically very far apart, he never knew what she really felt and thought as she was growing up—about him, about Rupert. He'd taken it for granted that since he'd always been careful to show an interest in what she did, had been there for advice and encouragement, and since she'd never gone materially short of anything, she must be happy. And she

had been happy, or at least she hadn't been unhappy. Until she met Rupert, and found out what unhappiness really was.

Don't cry. Don't show it when you're hurt. Control yourself, even when you feel you're going to burst with happiness, and love . . .

"God, you're a cold-hearted bitch!" Rupert had accused her, not having the nous or the sensitivity or whatever it needed to see that she couldn't, however she tried, lay herself open by admitting how he could set her on fire.

But now the dam had burst. The murky waters of emotion boiled and swirled around her. She felt she was drowning in them and had to fight to come to the surface. She'd begun to shiver, uncontrollably, feeling premonitions of further disasters to come, and she said suddenly, "I'm so cold, I'll make some tea. Do you want some?"

"I'd rather have hot cocoa."

It was a funny old time of day for cocoa. But yes, why not? What did the usual conventions matter? "Yes, cocoa, that's a good idea."

So she went down the familiar draughty passage to the kitchen Mrs. Stretton had left neat as a new pin and boiled milk and made some in the old blue jug, putting mugs on a tray and carrying it back carefully. A physical comfort that could do nothing to allay the rapidly mounting terror inside. That they should sit calmly drinking cocoa while the catastrophic happenings of the last few days hung between them was as unreal as everything else about the afternoon, irrational as the things one did in dreams. But this was a nightmare from which she would never wake up.

Without looking directly at him, she was aware of him observing her from under his heavy brows, his knotted hands busy with his pipe. When she'd seen him the other day on his birthday after so long an interval, she'd been shocked and dismayed to see how old he looked, how gaunt the intervening years had made him. But he'd lost none of his disciplined severity, and knowing that she was still, as always, overawed by his forcefulness, she had to make herself speak.

"You know—about Rupert, Father, don't you?" She couldn't bring herself to be more plain, but there, it was out. And his answer, when it came, was as indirect as her question. He reached into his pocket for his rubber pouch, refilled and lit his pipe, his actions deliberate and unhurried, before he spoke, calm and apparently un-worried.

"It's all one now. Water under the bridge. Don't worry, we'll make out, yet."

We. The two of them, together again, but now linked by death. What had she done, what had she brought on them? She knew by her father's face that *he* knew—and didn't blame her for it, either.

"I think we have to talk," he said. "Get things straight between us. It'll soon be too late."

She felt no shock because she'd become used to the idea of what must be during the last few days, but she did feel a sudden, over-whelming revulsion at the thought of facing it. Already regretting what she'd started, panicking, she put down her mug so fiercely that what remained of its contents splashed over the top, and stood up, startling Minty, who growled and got to her feet too. "No, I don't want to talk. That's something we should've done years ago. It's too late now. I think I'd much better go home."

"Sit down, Georgina. Sit, Minty."

And such was the habit of obedience they sat down, the woman and the dog.

The mellow old clock chimed a quarter to the hour. The dog was restless, knowing it was time for her walk. "I'd better take her," Culver said. "It won't take long. But before I do, I want you to listen to me."

"Don't leave me, Father. I'll come with you." Anything was better than sitting here alone.

"No!" The old man's voice was harsh. "You'll wait here, girl." He stroked the bitch's restless head until she settled on the rug again, then looked at his daughter, his face creased with the effort to find the right words. Lamely, for him, he said, "Everything will be all right, Georgina," then drew on his pipe and began to speak.

Outside, rain spattered briefly against the windows and then stopped. Inside the quiet room, his harsh voice rose and fell and soon, mingling with it, her swift, clipped accents.

Hours later, it seemed, though it was barely half an hour, she heard the sound of tyres hissing on the wet tarmac of the drive. It was with a sense of inevitability that she looked through the window and saw the police.

She took them into the study, resenting their intrusion into this private place, but having nowhere else other than the kitchen. The two men and the pretty, confidently efficient young policewoman seemed tall and menacing in the close confines of the small room, especially the Chief Inspector, whose grey eyes, steady and watchful, never left her face.

How, she wondered, was she going to get through this, knowing what she did and being more than a little frightened of him, of that sense of pent-up energy that was no less formidable for being kept severely in check. She wondered if he'd any idea how he affected people, or perhaps it was only those who were guilty who felt as she had at their previous interviews, as if she hardly dare speak for fear of having her words pounced on and only too correctly interpreted.

"Where's your father, Mrs. Fleming?" were his first, hardly intimidating, words.

"He's taken Minty for her walk. He won't be long."

"Then perhaps we can take the opportunity of a few words with you until he gets back."

"I thought we'd said all we have to say."

"Oh, not by a long chalk," he said easily. "And I think you know that, don't you? Are you going to be honest with me, now that you've had time to think it over?"

She knew that she'd no other choice, after her talk with her father, and after a short struggle with herself, recalling her promises to him, she finally relinquished her defences and gave up. And having given up, it suddenly seemed easier. She asked tonelessly what it was he wanted to know.

"Begin with the last time you saw your husband, and go on from there."

Despite the cold, the daffodil buds were bursting, spreading in a sheet of greeny-gold under the birches. On the bare elms, the buds were fat and red, giving a rosy haze to the trees. As Culver whistled for the dog and turned to make his way over the rough grass in the direction of the quarry, a yellowhammer sang its "little-bit-of-bread-and-no-cheese" song in the hedge.

Reaching the rim of the quarry, Culver paused. "Sit."

The dog sat, obedient and expectant, head cocked to one side, looking at him with alert, intelligent eyes, the same colour as Georgina's. Culver closed his own eyes for a moment, then raised the gun and tightened his finger on the trigger.

"The last time I saw him," Georgina said rapidly, "was Monday evening, about eight o'clock, but I knew something was wrong before then. I knew as soon as I saw him that Sunday. He was so keyed up, you could almost feel it. His eyes were sort of glittering and he couldn't keep still. If I hadn't known Rupert better, I'd have thought he was high on something . . ."

Mayo was shocked by her appearance. When they'd first come into the room, he'd thought she seemed as usual, the rag-doll hair, the pearly-pale face and the drooping poppy mouth. Now he noticed that her nail varnish was slightly chipped, one of her blouse buttons was undone and the flat, scuffed shoes looked as though they were ones she kept for driving and had forgotten to change. There were deep shadows under her eyes. But most of all it was her manner, all the unbending self-control gone.

". . . perhaps he was high on his own excitement," she went on. "He could hardly contain himself, but it wasn't until—until late in the evening that he told me what it was all about. He said he was in trouble, terrible trouble, and he'd have to get away. Well, of course, it was money he wanted, it always was, and in the end I promised I'd let him have some, as I always did. I've always been a fool where Rupert was concerned."

This was at least twice as long as any speech he'd ever heard her make. It was a big admission, too. He said nothing, not wanting to interrupt her now she had at last broken her self-imposed silence, willing her to go on.

"We agreed that I'd get the money the following day and he'd come and pick it up. But during the day I had time to do some thinking. I didn't know what kind of trouble he was in, but it seemed to me the time had come for him to face up to things.

Somebody had always made out for him, usually me, and he never was going to amount to anything if I went on doing so. So when he came, I told him I hadn't got the money."

"How did he react to that?"

"He went nearly crazy." She blinked rapidly several times. "I'd never seen him rant and rave like that. He really seemed—quite mad. And then, that was when he told me why he needed the money, and why he had to get away. It seems that"—her voice faltered—"well, it seems he'd been involved with Ashleigh Cockayne down at the Gaiety in some tacky little scheme to make money out of photographs . . . which I suppose you know all about?"

"Some of it. You may be able to fill me in on the details later."

She shook her crimped bob. "That was the first I knew of it. But I realized it must have been questionable, because he told me one of your policemen had come snooping around- -that was what he called it. And there'd been a fight. And the policeman died. And he and Cockayne had put his body into the river." She spoke as if she were being driven by some force she couldn't contain, glossing over the appalling events in a flat, rapid monotone, as if that might make them less appalling. "But Cockayne panicked, he said the body was sure to turn up, and what then? He said he was going to go to the police to report what had happened, tell them it was an accident. Rupert told him he was out of his mind if he thought they'd believe that."

Kite said, "It was no accident."

Georgina turned to look at him blankly, as though one of the pieces of furniture had spoken. "I know," she said. "I know, it couldn't have been. That's why Rupert was so scared. He *was* scared, one hundred percent. It seemed to me he'd gone right over the top. He was really wild, he didn't seem to care anymore what he'd done. Well, we argued for over an hour, but I was determined not to give in, and in the end he left."

"And that was the last time you saw him?"

"Yes." She avoided his eyes.

He left it and came back to an earlier point of contention. "You identified the body in the mortuary as your husband's. Knowing that it was the body of Ashleigh Cockayne."

"That was so horrible!" She shivered, drawing herself together. "I knew it wasn't Rupert, but I saw in a flash what must have happened, that he must have shot Cockayne. That's what he'd been planning, that was why he wanted the money to get away. So I said it was Rupert. It couldn't do Cockayne any harm, he was dead, and Rupert . . . well, he was still my husband. Maybe it was partly my fault, what had happened. If I'd given him the money . . . maybe I owed him this last thing. I didn't see any reason why anybody should ever know what I'd done."

"A lot of people have thought that in the past, Mrs. Fleming," Mayo said. "Where is your husband now?"

"I don't know," she said.

"You don't know?" He knew that to be a lie. "Well, before your father comes back, suppose we talk about the Volkswagen belonging to Ashleigh Cockayne. I must tell you we've spoken to Mr. Tim Salisbury, who's admitted how he got rid of it—"

At that moment, there was the slam of a shotgun, followed by another.

For several minutes Culver had kept the gun raised. At last he pressed the trigger. Minty fell but he didn't look at her. Keeping his eyes on the distant skyline, he prepared to fire the second barrel. And then at the last moment he swung round, releasing into the air the shot intended for himself.

Too many deaths already, too much grief. Fleming wasn't going to win that way.

He dropped the gun and slowly bent to pick up the bitch. Carrying her in his arms, he strode back to the house where Georgina, and the police, were waiting.

"Mr. Culver, I'll ask you the question I've been asking your daughter, and hope I get a more satisfactory answer. I have to ask you, what has happened to Rupert Fleming?"

Culver sat in the wing chair by the fire, impassive as an Easter Island statue. "What makes you think I should know that?"

"For one thing, you sent money to the woman he was living with.

A thousand pounds in five-pound notes, which you put into an unsealed letter you found in his pocket and then posted . . ."

"That's pure guesswork!" But the momentary flicker of his eyes showed him as surprised as he would ever allow himself to be.

"Ever heard of genetic fingerprinting, Mr. Culver? It won't be guesswork that proves it's your saliva on the envelope and stamp, and your prints on the money and the envelope. And I'm satisfied there's only one way you could have got at that letter. He's dead, isn't he?"

Culver smiled sardonically, but Mayo thought he detected some subtle change in his attitude. Defeat? No, not yet. "I'm surprised you don't know, seeing you know so much otherwise."

"Don't get clever with me, Mr. Culver. I want to know what happened on the night Ashleigh Cockayne was murdered."

The old man filled his pipe, lit it and said nothing. It seemed evident he was prepared to stall all night, if necessary. He looked tired, though. His heavy shoulders drooped and his sharp eyes had lost some of their alertness. He had cleaned up after bringing the dog home, but there was a smear of blood that he'd missed across the back of his wrist.

"If you won't say, then let's talk about something else. The gun that killed Cockayne belonged to you. You claimed it'd been stolen, but there was no evidence of forced entry." He spoke to Georgina. "Mrs. Fleming, when you left home on your marriage, did you keep the keys you presumably had to this house?"

"My father never asked me to return them. Did you, Father?"

"Of course I didn't, girl, of course I didn't. Still your home, wasn't it?"

"Did your husband know you had them?"

"He might have."

"Either he did, and used them to obtain the twelve-bore with which he shot Ashleigh Cockayne, or you yourself got the gun for him."

"No!" Georgina said, simultaneously with Culver's harsh "Don't be a fool!"

"All right," Mayo said, "I'm satisfied it *was* Fleming who took the keys and got the gun. And assuming that was so, it seems logical to me to assume that when Cockayne's car wouldn't start—in which Fleming had intended making a break after shooting Cockayne—he would think of yours, not very far away in a garage to which he had the keys. I think he walked up over the hill and through the wood behind the house, intending to take your car and then drive back to pick up his belongings from the Volkswagen. Unfortunately for him, he never did get back. I have to ask you, Mr. Culver, did you kill Rupert Fleming?"

Georgina jumped up with an exclamation and crossed the room to sit on the arm of her father's chair. She laid a hand on his sleeve. "It wasn't as you think," she began, but her father stopped her with a firm hand over hers.

"I'd no choice," he said suddenly. "I did kill him, yes—in a manner of speaking. But I'd no choice and I've no regrets. He was a murderer, he'd killed two men, one in anger, one in cold blood. There was no future for him, anyway."

P.C.W. Platt looked up from her pad. Her eyes were wide. She'd never been in at a murder confession before. Certainly not one as cold and matter-of-fact as this promised to be. Her pencil began to fly again as Culver went on.

"He came here at one o'clock in the morning. I was just going to bed when I heard someone moving about outside in the yard at the back. I turned the light out and drew back the curtains on one of the side windows and I saw a man fiddling with the door of the old barn where I keep my car. I got my gun and went out at the back door and round to the side. He heard me and when he turned round I saw it was Rupert Fleming."

"Did you shoot him?"

"No, I did not. I demanded an explanation of what he was doing, though it was pretty obvious he wouldn't have been there if he hadn't been intending to make off with my car. He said he had to get away, he was in bad trouble. He asked me for money . . . money—from *me!*" Culver laughed harshly. "I asked him, 'What makes you think I would give *you* money?' 'You would if you knew the whole story,' he said. 'Then you'd better tell it to me.'"

A log fell in the fire. Culver leaned forward and pushed it together, sat back and puffed at his pipe before resuming talking as coolly as though he were telling some mildly interesting anecdote. "He wanted to come inside, but I told him to stay where he was. He was uneasy because I had the gun on him, but he told me the whole sorry tale . . . well, I don't suppose there's any need to repeat that. The upshot was that he needed money and some means of getting away. He knew I always kept cash in the house and then he got cocky and said if I didn't give it him he'd take it anyway. 'You wouldn't shoot me,' he said, 'think of the scandal to your precious daughter.' The fool, threatening me like that. Didn't he realize I didn't need to kill him, I was armed and I could easily have disabled him? But then he made his mistake. He raised his hand to me. He shouldn't have done that, not with Minty by my side."

At the mention of his dog, Culver paused, an involuntary spasm that might have been pain crossing his face, but when he resumed he was as much in control as before. "He put his hands on my shoulders and began to shake me. Minty went for his heels. He staggered and we both fell. I found myself lying on top of him with my hands round his neck. He tried to pull me off but Minty got her teeth into his hand. And then, all of a sudden, I knew he was dead."

The sound of Jenny Platt flipping a page of her notebook over was like a whiplash in the silence.

"Where is he now?"

"Under the flagstones in the tower. I gave myself a shot of brandy and after a while I dragged him outside. It wasn't difficult, I've always kept myself fit."

Georgina got up and faced him. Her voice strangled, she said, "That money they say you sent, Father . . . why didn't you tell me about that?"

Culver turned in his chair to face his daughter. "I hoped that might not be necessary, girl."

"But why? Why did you send it? To—to *her!*"

"I went through his pockets and got my keys back and I saw the letter. It wasn't sealed and I read it. It appeared from what he wrote that he'd been intending to send her money and it seemed hard to me that she shouldn't have any. She'd had a bad-enough time with him already, so I left the letter as it was, put some cash in and posted it."

"You knew about her?" The bewilderment in her voice, so unlike her, did more than anything to make Mayo feel pity for her.

"I've always," Culver replied harshly, "made it my business to know everything about Fleming. I knew one day the score would even itself out, though I never intended it to happen the way it did." He turned from his daughter and spoke to Mayo. "I'm prepared to pay for what I've done, but I'd just like to repeat that I don't regret anything except the sorrow I've caused my daughter."

With a dry catch in her throat, Georgina tried to speak.

"Cry, girl, cry, it'll do you good," Culver said.

But now, after all this time, she couldn't.

Mayo stood up, ready to make the formal caution. He was surprised at how quickly Culver had given in, but glad of it, knowing that without his confession they could never have proved his guilt, might never have known what had happened to Rupert Fleming. With a plea of self-defence, he might be lucky and get away with manslaughter.

Father and daughter stood before him, Culver gaunt and ruined, aged by ten years, Georgina looking bereft. It's bizarre, Mayo thought, sickened. All this sudden disruption to so many lives . . . all these deaths.

But no more so, perhaps, than life itself.

About the Author

Marjorie Eccles has written several romance novels under two pseud-
onyms (Judith Bordill and Jennifer Hyde). This is her fourth novel
for the Crime Club. She lives in Berkhamsted, England.